Praise for Kate Hoffmann's The Mighty Quinns

"[Kate] Hoffmann always brings a strong story to the table with The Mighty Quinns, and this is one of her best."
—*RT Book Reviews* on *The Mighty Quinns: Eli*

"The [Aileen Quinn storyline] ends as it began: with strong storytelling and compelling, tender characters who make for a deeply satisfying read."
—*RT Book Reviews* on *The Mighty Quinns: Mac*

"[Hoffmann's] characters are well written and real. *The Mighty Quinns: Eli* is a recommended read for lovers of the Quinn family, lovers of the outdoors and lovers of a sensitive man."
—*Harlequin Junkie*

"A winning combination of exciting adventure and romance... This is a sweet and sexy read that kept me entertained from start to finish."
—*Harlequin Junkie* on *The Mighty Quinns: Malcolm*

"Ms. Hoffmann's voice is smooth, calming and soulful.... If you are looking for a steamy romance with an engaging storyline, give this book a try."
—*Harlequin Junkie* on *The Mighty Quinns: Roarke*

"*The Mighty Quinns: Jack* is one of those stories that will capture your mind and heat your emotions. It was impossible for me to put this steamy, sexy book down until the last page was turned."
—*Fresh Fiction*

Dear Reader,

One of the best things about being a writer is creating interesting characters. Sometimes those characters live entirely on the pages of my books, but other times they seem to come to life in my mind. They almost seem real. And I enjoy their company so much that when I finish the book, I actually feel a bit lonely for these temporary "guests."

The Mighty Quinns: Tristan was one of those books that brought together an odd community of characters that really stayed with me long after the book was finished. I hope you enjoy them as much as I did!

Happy reading,

Kate Hoffmann

Kate Hoffmann

The Mighty Quinns: Tristan

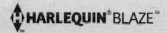

HARLEQUIN® BLAZE™

Recycling programs
for this product may
not exist in your area.

ISBN-13: 978-0-373-79917-6

The Mighty Quinns: Tristan

Printed in U.S.A.

HARLEQUIN®
www.Harlequin.com

Kate Hoffmann lives in southeastern Wisconsin with her books, her computer and her cats, Princess Winifred and Princess Grace. In her spare time she enjoys sewing, baking, movies, theater and talking on the phone with her sister. She has written nearly ninety books for Harlequin.

Books by Kate Hoffmann

Harlequin Blaze

Seducing the Marine
Compromising Positions

The Mighty Quinns

The Mighty Quinns: Rourke
The Mighty Quinns: Dex
The Mighty Quinns: Malcolm
The Mighty Quinns: Rogan
The Mighty Quinns: Ryan
The Mighty Quinns: Eli
The Mighty Quinns: Devin
The Mighty Quinns: Mac
The Mighty Quinns: Thom

To get the inside scoop on Harlequin Blaze and its talented writers, visit Facebook.com/BlazeAuthors.

All backlist available in ebook format.

Visit the Author Profile page at Harlequin.com for more titles.

To Judge Andy S. for helping with legal matters.

Prologue

THEY'D LIVED IN the blue house on Downey Street for just five months. Tristan had been so excited to move in. A real house after the family of five had spent their summer living in the car or sleeping in a tent. But when his father had died and the cold weather set in, things became desperate again.

They scraped together just enough money to survive from panhandling, petty theft and their mother's disability payments. The Quinns couldn't pay their rent, but no one wanted to evict tenants in the middle of winter. That was what their mother depended upon— the guilt of strangers.

Tristan stood at the window, scraping his finger over the frost that coated the inside. The heat and the electricity had been turned off two months ago. They'd been forced to depend upon a smoky fireplace for warmth and a gas-station restroom for water and plumbing facilities.

"Where is she?" Tristan's little brother, Jamie, asked.

Their mother had taken their other brother, Thom,

out to pinch some food from the local market. They'd been caught last month stealing a box of cereal, but the store owner had refused to press charges during the holiday season. He'd sent them home with a huge box of food that had lasted nearly a week.

Up and down. That was the way life seemed to work for the Quinns. Just when things started looking a little better, something would knock them down.

Tristan rubbed his arms through his jacket, his breath clouding in front of his face. His mother and Thom had been gone far too long. Something had happened, and Tristan was afraid of the consequences.

They were always just a few steps ahead of CPS—Child Protective Services—the dragon that loomed over their small world, waiting to snatch one or all of them away. Tristan couldn't go to the police to find his mother because they'd discover that he and his brothers were alone, living in an unheated house in the middle of a Minnesota winter. And then CPS would separate them, possibly forever. So he and his brothers were forced to wait and wonder where their mother was—sometimes for a day or two, sometimes, if she managed to score some booze or drugs, for weeks.

The sound of footsteps on the porch caught Tristan's attention and he held his breath, wondering who it might be. Burglars regularly broke into the house, looking for anything worth selling. The landlord made threatening appearances occasionally.

"Hey!"

Jamie smiled. "Thom," he said.

A few seconds later, the second of the three Quinn

brothers strolled in, his jacket unzipped, his face red from the cold. He carried a crumpled grocery bag, which he dropped on the floor next to the fireplace.

"What happened?"

"I told her she shouldn't take the booze. She was already drunk, you'd think she could do without it for once. She was walking out and she dropped a bottle. It shattered around her feet. I grabbed what I could and ran, but they got her. She's probably in jail now."

"We have to rescue her," Jamie said.

"No," Tristan replied. "No. She's safe there. She'll have food, and a bed and heat. They won't let her drink. If we go get her there'll be too many questions. You know I'm right, don't you, Jamie?"

The younger boy nodded.

"We'll survive just fine on our own," Tristan explained. "We have a fire and something to eat. We've got our sleeping bags to keep us extra warm. It will be like camping. And in the morning, we'll go to school and we'll be warm for the whole day and have a hot meal. We'll make it through. We always do."

Tristan reached out and pulled Jamie into his arms, giving him a hug. Then he looked over at Thom. "Why don't you eat? I'm going to see if I can find some more wood for the fire. I passed a house on my way to school that had stacks of firewood. If I can take some, we'll be warm for a few days."

"It's really cold out," Thom warned. "Wear the red coat. That has a good hood."

Tristan left his brothers in front of the fire, picking through the bag of snacks that Thom had managed to steal. Tris bundled up against the cold, then headed out, turning toward the alley that ran between the blocks of houses in their run-down neighborhood.

As he walked, he sniffed the air for the scent of a fire, squinting into the sky for a curl of smoke that might come from a nearby chimney.

Everything looked so different in the dark, especially when covered with a layer of white. But he found a house with a fire burning inside. He peered through the windows into the darkened interior, noticing the bars that blocked his entrance. But to his surprise, a side door to the garage had been left open, probably so the owner could retrieve more wood.

"This is good," he murmured with a smile. Now he just had to find a way to carry it home. He could balance three, maybe four pieces in his hands. Not enough even for the night. He needed a way to move more wood.

The light from the alley allowed him to see the interior of the garage. He spotted a tarp and a wheelbarrow. Tristan grabbed the tarp. The wheelbarrow would be missed and he wasn't sure he was strong enough to push it, but he could easily drag the tarp through the snow.

Tristan made quick work of the task, knowing the longer he took, the greater the odds of being caught. He managed to load up sixteen logs before he carefully closed the door and headed down the alley.

The guy would never miss the wood and Tristan's family would be warm for the next day or two. He didn't feel bad about stealing. Guilt was no longer an emotion he could afford. But every time he'd been forced to break the law or take advantage of someone to survive, Tristan made a promise to himself.

One day, when he was older, when he no longer had to take care of his brothers and they were on their own, he'd find a way to help people who were in trouble or struggling to survive.

He'd find them food or a nice place to live or maybe a job that would help to buy clothes and an ice cream cone every now and then. He wasn't sure what kind of job it would be, but if there was something like that in the world, he'd find it...

_1_

TRISTAN QUINN DOWN-SHIFTED the sleek silver convertible as he navigated the narrow curve of the road. Dappled sunlight filtered through the trees lining each side of the pavement, the thick green forest broken only by occasional homemade signs indicating cottages and resorts located deep within the woods.

He drew a deep breath, enjoying the brisk wind and warm sun on his face. There were moments when he had to wonder why he'd decided to seek a career in law, except for the rather sizable salary. He could have easily enjoyed being a construction worker or a ditch digger. At least he'd be free of the confines of his office, free to enjoy the weather, the warm summer days and even the bitter cold that came with the winters in Minneapolis.

So when this case had come up, Tristan had jumped at the opportunity. Though the matter had plagued most of the lawyers in his office, it meant an entire day outside of the office. He'd left that morning, headed northwest, a tidy stack of documents tucked in his briefcase. Today, he'd take his shot at negotiating a settlement to a contentious real estate case that had been going on for three long years.

Though most of the lawyers in the firm had worked on the case, this was his first crack at it. It was his chance to show the partners what he could do.

The case involved a dispute over an incredibly beautiful piece of land located an hour from the city on a pristine and very private lake. It was one of the only undeveloped lakes that close to Minneapolis–St. Paul, and as such was considered gold for any real estate developer.

The land had been held by the Pigglestone Family Trust since the late 1950s, and since then had been the site of an artists' colony. But the latest generation wanted to sell the land, and in order to do that, they needed to evict their three elderly aunts, who had lived on the property from the beginning. Papers had been drawn up, notices sent, but the women had largely ignored the court orders.

Tristan didn't relish evicting a trio of old ladies, but the partners had authorized him to offer an extraordinary financial settlement—one that would set the women up in relative luxury almost anywhere in the world. Though the job had proved impossible for others, Tristan was confident he'd be able to complete this task in a day or two and return to the firm a winner. After all, he'd been charming women for as long as he as he could remember.

"Turn right, two hundred yards."

He glanced over at the navigation screen and frowned. He hadn't seen any road signs for the past mile and assumed that he was off the grid. But a few moments later the voice warned him again. "Turn right, one hundred yards."

He slowed the car and watched for a sign. But all that was visible was thick brush and tall trees. "Turn right, twenty yards."

The narrow side road suddenly appeared and Tristan slammed on the brakes in order to make the turn. There was no sign or any indication of what lay ahead. But the coordinates had come directly from his boss so he knew he could trust them.

As he drove deeper into the woods, the road narrowed until it was only wide enough for one car to pass. Tristan slowly rounded a curve but skidded to a stop when he saw a figure standing in the middle of the road.

Her arms were stretched above her head, her fingers spread wide. She stood perfectly still, only the breeze moving her hair. She wore a loose cotton blouse that barely covered her backside—and nothing else. Tristan watched her for a long moment, his gaze drifting lower to take in the sweet curve of her naked backside. He couldn't see her face, but somehow he sensed that she would be beautiful.

She continued to watch the trees above her head and then suddenly her hands drifted down to her sides. Tristan switched off the car and waited, remaining still and silent, afraid he might spook her. She tilted her head slightly as if she'd caught some sound deep in the woods. Finally, her shoulders dropped and she slowly shook her head.

When she turned to face him, his suspicions were proven true. She was beautiful. Breathtakingly beautiful. Like some wild wood nymph, her dark tousled hair fell in curls around perfect features.

"This is private property," she called, bracing her hands on her waist. The cotton shirt lifted again, revealing the tops of her shapely legs. His gaze drifted down to her bare feet, which were covered with mud.

Tristan got out of the car, closing the door behind him before he approached. "What were you looking for?"

"I wasn't looking," she said. "I was listening."

"Then what were you listening for?"

"An owl. A great gray owl. Every now and then when I walk along this stretch of road, I hear him. I just can't tell where the sound is coming from. Maybe it's just the wind playing tricks on my ears. Or maybe it's a ghost."

"What does he sound like?" Tristan asked.

"I'm not very good at bird calls," she said.

"Give it a try. I'm curious."

"Actually, it sounds just like sex."

"Sex?"

"Yeah. It's kind of a soft, grunting sound. Uh, uh, uh."

"I thought owls said 'who,'" Tristan joked.

"That's only in cartoons," she murmured. "I once saw a red-necked grebe. That's very rare for this area. Indigo buntings are my favorite, but hard to spot.

They're the most beautiful shade of blue, but not really indigo at all." She met his gaze. "Closer to lapis. Or azure. Are you lost?" she asked. "Can I help you?"

A little dazed by her quick change in subject matter, Tristan tried to refocus on the task at hand. "I'm looking for this old artists' colony. I read about it and wanted to check it out."

"An artists' colony? I've never heard of anything like that," she said. "Are you sure you're in the right place? There's nothing but cottages at the end of this road."

"I'm certain," he said. "Fence Lake Artists' Colony. It was founded in the fifties. By three sisters?" He met her gaze. "None of this sounds familiar?"

She shook her head. "Nope."

Tristan knew she was lying. He'd never met a beautiful woman who was a decent liar. Hell, he could read any woman, gorgeous or Plain Jane, in half the time he could read a man. It was one of the talents that made him a great litigator.

Well, if she was going to lie, then he'd be forced to counter her deception with one of his own. "Hmm. That's too bad. I was really hoping I could spend a week or so there."

"You're an artist?"

He nodded. "Writer. I'm not published, but I have a publisher interested in my book. I need to rewrite part of it and I'm blocked. I was hoping a new environment would help." He glanced over his shoulder at his car. "I should probably get going. I must have taken a wrong turn somewhere."

She stared at him for a long moment. Yes, she definitely knew much more than she was willing to reveal. But how much? "I suppose I could help you out," she murmured.

"You have a map?"

"I can take you to the colony," she said. "I'm staying there myself."

"Are you a writer?"

"Artist," she said. "Painter. Sculptor. Whatever medium and subject catches my attention. Lately, it's been owls."

"I don't want to take you away from your bird-watching," he said.

She shrugged. "'In every walk with nature, one receives far more than he seeks.'" She smiled. "John Muir. Do you mind if I drive? The road is a bit tricky."

Tristan shook his head. "I don't even know your name. Why would I let you drive my car?"

"Because the road is very curvy and narrow. I wouldn't want you to wreck your car." She held out her hand. "Lily Harrison."

Tristan held his breath as he tried to hide his surprise. He'd been warned about this woman. But he'd never expected her to be so young—or beautiful.

Lily Alicia Hopkins Harrison. Her mother was heir to the Pigglestone fortune and her father heir to the Harrison fortune. But instead of following in her parents' footsteps, Lily had become an artist, activist and protector of the three Pigglestone sisters. Meanwhile her family had hired his law firm to convince the elderly sisters to vacate the land.

Last summer, Lily and the aunts had chained them-selves to the porches of their cottages when the bull-dozers had arrived to demolish the colony. She'd appeared in the news media and marshalled her forces on social media to make the rest of the family look like greedy Scrooges trying to toss three old women out of their homes.

"Have you ever had an accident?" he asked. "Any speeding tickets?"

"No to both," she said.

"May I see your license?"

"I don't have one," she said. "Never got one. But I drive really well."

"How do you get around?"

"I make do," she said with a shrug.

Right. Her first car had probably been a limousine.

"It's a pleasure to meet you," he said, taking her hand. "I'm—I'm Quinn. Quinn James." His brother's name was the first that came to mind. It would have been too easy for her to Google his name and find out he worked for the very law firm that had been causing her trouble. With an alias, he could hopefully maintain his anonymity long enough to get to the three aunts and make his proposal. After that, it wouldn't matter.

"That's a good name for a writer," she said. "What kind of book are you writing?"

Since that was another lie, he decided to change the subject. "I'd love to see some of your work. You said you painted owls?"

"No," she said. "Owls have just been on my mind lately. They visit me in my dreams. I think it's a sign but I'm not sure what it means. Do you know what it might mean?"

He slowly shook his head. "I'm afraid I don't." Tristan walked to the car and opened the driver's-side door, waiting for her to slip behind the wheel.

So far, things had gone much easier than he'd imagined they might. However, his problems were mounting. Now, if he managed to wrangle an invitation to stay at the colony, he'd have to produce a novel—or at least a few pages. But his biggest test was still the three sisters.

He circled the car and jumped into the passenger seat. He'd cross that bridge when he came to it. For now he was determined to get to know this strange yet beautiful woman. He sensed that Lily might be the key to everything he wanted—both professionally and personally.

"HE'S A LAWYER. I'd be willing to bet my life on it."

Lily paced the length of her aunt Violet's front parlor. Violet, dressed in her usual dance attire of black unitard and chiffon skirt, casually sipped at her tea. Her gray curls were covered by an elaborately tied scarf and her eyes were ringed with dark makeup. "Do sit down, Lily. I think your imagination has run away with you again."

"I'm right, I'm sure of it. He says he's a writer, but no writer I've met would drive a car like that. A Mercedes convertible? In Minnesota? Do you know what that car says?"

"I wasn't aware automobiles had acquired the power of speech."

Lily rolled her eyes. "You understand what I meant."

"Please, Lily, be more precise in your speech. If you don't stop this tendency of yours to wander off topic, you're going to start sounding like Daisy. Trying to follow her train of thought is like chasing a hummingbird through the woods."

"I'm not going off topic. That expensive convertible says that he's a lawyer. It tells anyone who bothers to notice that he's wealthy enough to have a summer and a winter car. And then there are his shoes. And his watch."

"Perhaps he's a lawyer who is attempting to be a writer," her aunt suggested. "Must you always be so suspicious? Not everyone is out to get us."

"I'm just trying to protect us all," Lily said.

The door to Violet's cabin opened and her two sisters hurried inside. Rose, the youngest of the trio, wore her long gray hair in an untidy knot on the top of her head. A composer, she was currently working on a new series of songs inspired by art. Over the course of the day, she'd stuck pencils in her hair until she looked like some deranged geisha.

The middle sister, Daisy, was an artist like Lily and could normally be found wearing a paint-stained smock and a scarf covering her hair, which had been dyed a shocking shade of pink for the last few months. Before that, it had been lavender, a much more appropriate tone for someone of her age.

"What is the problem?" Daisy asked. "I really need

to get back to work. Did you see the sunrise this morning?" She sighed. "Paris, 1963."

Violet motioned for them to sit down. "Lily thinks she's seen a lawyer. Here. At the colony."

"What? Just wandering through?" Rose asked.

"No," Lily said. "He's pretending to be a writer. He's asked to stay."

"What do you call those clouds that look like horse's tails?" Daisy asked.

"I'm not sure," Lily said. "I suspect he's going to try to get closer to you three."

"He's welcome to try, but you know we can't be persuaded," Violet said. "Nothing he says will change our mind. We're not going to leave the colony and that's that."

"Then what do you want me to do about him?" Lily asked.

"Well, perhaps we should take him in," Violet said. "We might find him useful for other reasons. And don't they say that it's better to keep your friends close and your enemies closer?"

"Who said that?" Rose asked. "I do recall arguing about that very quote one night at the bar in the Savoy Hotel in London. I'd had far too many gin fizzes."

"Wilbur Fontaine," Daisy said.

"Who?"

"The butcher in town," Daisy explained. "I heard him say that very thing just last month. 'Keep your friends close and your enemies closer.' Or maybe it was 'keep your musket cocked and your tinder dry.' But I'm not really sure what that means."

Violet sighed softly. "Back to the matter at hand... We could be like cats with a mouse with this lawyer. When we grow tired of him, we'll send him home. We haven't had real amusement here in such a very long time. Let's do ask him to stay."

"I asked Finch to take him on a tour of the colony while we talked," Lily said. "He's supposed to bring Quinn back here for tea when they're finished. But we should have our plans in place before he gets here."

"How old is he?" Rose asked.

"I suppose he's about my age," Lily replied.

The aunts looked at each other and smiled. "And is he handsome?" Violet asked Lily.

"No, he looks like a lawyer," Lily said, "one of those shrewd, ruthless types who eat people like us for breakfast."

"Oh, he can't be that bad. Even a lawyer has to have some redeeming qualities."

"They can get you out of jail when you've started a brawl at the Opera Ball and slapped a policeman's horse," Daisy said.

"I'm sure, given time, the three of us can noodle the truth out of him," Violet said.

A knock sounded on the screen door and Violet stood up, tucking a strand of hair behind her ear and beneath her scarf. "Well, shall we have a look at Lily's lawyer?"

Lily held her breath as her aunt walked to the door. A few moments later, Mr. Quinn James stepped inside. He had an easy way of moving that made all eyes in the room follow him. Lily could see immediately that even her aunts found him attractive. What was it about him?

Was it the nearly black hair that looked as though he had just gotten out of bed? His face was a perfect balance of features, so composed that a search for any flaw was impossible. Or was it his voice? Deep and warm and so sexy that it made her heart beat just a tiny bit faster with every word that he spoke.

Violet held out her hand, arching her wrist and waiting for the customary kiss rather than a polite shake. Lily was surprised that he took the cue and touched his lips to a spot just above her fingers.

"It's a pleasure to meet you, Miss Violet."

Violet introduced her sisters and Quinn kissed their outstretched hands, as well.

"Quinn James, at your service," he said. He sat down next to Lily, his thigh brushing against hers. Warmth seeped into her bare leg and she found her attention fixed on the spot, her pulse pounding in her head.

"Where are you from, Mr. James?" Violet asked.

"Call me Quinn," he said. "The Twin Cities. I was born in St. Paul. I've lived there all my life."

"And how long have you been writing?" Rose asked.

"Five years, on and off. I've only just decided that it's something I really want to pursue."

"Lily tells us you'd like to stay with us for a while," Rose said.

"I'm not sure that we have an opening," Lily interrupted. "You may have to share a cabin. And we rarely take unpublished writers. Unless, of course, we have a chance to read their work first."

"Now, darling, I'm sure we can find him a suitable place to stay. After all, he has important work to do." Violet fixed her gaze on him.

"There is the other side of Finch's cabin," Rose suggested. "And I'm sure Finch would enjoy the company." Rose turned to smile at Quinn. "What say you, Mr. James? We'd be happy to have you stay."

"I don't mind sharing," he said.

"WELL DONE," VIOLET SAID. "Now that everything is settled, would you care for a cup of tea, Mr. James?"

Tristan was trying not to fist-pump. "Actually, I'd rather head back to the city right away," Tristan said. "I need to pack a few things."

"You didn't bring your things along?" Violet asked.

"I suppose I wasn't sure that you'd let me stay." He stood and gave them a smart bow. "But now that I am, I'm anxious to move in and get started. Ladies, I'll see you tomorrow."

"Do be sure to arrive by seven tomorrow night," Rose said. "Billy Farnsworth-Chadwick will be doing some scenes from Othello in our little theater, and he's asked Violet to dust off her Desdemona. She hasn't done that role since she was a stand-in opposite Olivier in London."

"I wouldn't miss it for the world," Quinn said.

Lily walked out the front door and held it open for him before they both went down the front steps. "I probably should've warned you about the aunts," she said.

"No," he said. "They're wonderful. Did she actually play opposite Laurence Olivier on the stage?"

"You can never be sure with the aunts," Lily said. "Sometimes their stories are true. And sometimes they're just wishful memories. I usually don't try to differentiate between the two. As long as they're happy, so am I."

When they reached the car, Tristan took her hand and pressed his lips against her wrist. A shiver skittered down her spine as the aftereffects of the simple kiss seeped through her bloodstream.

It had been a long time since a man had placed his lips on her body. And he hadn't been able to hide the fact that he was attracted to her. Surely there was some way she could make that work to her advantage.

For now she'd simply keep her eye on him. She'd find out the real reason for his appearance here and if he was working for the family, she'd send him packing.

"I suppose I'll see you tomorrow, then," said Lily.

"Is there anything you'd like me to bring you from the city?" Quinn asked.

"Not that I can think of," Lily said. "Just bring me something interesting to read. Your novel would be nice."

He chuckled softly before slipping behind the wheel and starting the car.

"Goodbye, Lily," he said.

"Goodbye, Quinn." Lily stepped back from the car and watched as he drove off, a small cloud of dust trailing after him.

She would have to keep a clear head if she was going to figure out his motives. He was quite a charmer, and she'd have to keep her wits about her. If he wasn't who he claimed to be, she'd find a way to expose him.

Expose him... Lily smiled to herself. It wasn't often that someone young and attractive wandered into camp, but Lily usually took advantage when it happened. A summer romance was always good for the creative juices. In the past, she'd done her best work while indulging in a little affair.

She shook her head. She had to remember that Quinn wasn't all he appeared to be. For now and the near future, she would keep Quinn at a safe distance.

She shivered, then rubbed her arms against the goose bumps that prickled her skin. It was at that moment she realized she wasn't wearing underwear beneath the loose cotton shift she wore.

Lily groaned, then turned and headed back to her cabin. She was used to running around in anything that she tossed on. With a dangerously attractive man nearby, she might actually have to put some thought into being more conservative with her wardrobe.

"LADIES AND GENTLEMEN, our firm has been working on this case for over three years and we have very little to show for it. The three sisters are still living happily on the property with no plans to vacate. I propose to get close to them, to live with them at the colony and find out what they really want. The big question I will answer is, what settlement would make them happy?"

Tristan scanned the conference room, searching for support for his unconventional idea. The law firm of Forster and Dunlap was not the kind of establishment that encouraged unconventional ideas. In fact, from the start, Tristan had felt like the odd man out among so many straightlaced and buttoned-up lawyers. But the firm had offered a start to a guy who was high on charisma and a little low on his law school GPA.

Getting through law school had been much tougher than Tristan had ever imagined. But then life had never been easy for him—or his two brothers. From a young age, they'd been forced to fend for themselves, first because their parents hadn't cared, then because their parents had abandoned them and then because they'd been in the foster care system.

He and Thom and Jamie had survived, but just how, he'd never been able to explain. Maybe it was the strength they'd found in each other, or the stubborn resolve they all had to survive and succeed.

He'd worked his way through college with the help of grants and odd jobs, but law school had been a different story. The expense and the expectations had almost killed him. He'd held down both a job and a full schedule of night school classes. That usually left no more than four or five hours to sleep at night.

But Tristan had been determined. At first, he had wanted to prove to the world that the eldest of Denny Quinn's boys was more than just a criminal's son. And then he'd needed to prove to himself that he was safe. That there would always be food in the refrigerator and a warm place to sleep.

He cleared his throat, waiting for some reaction from the partners in front of him. Sure, his idea was a little "out there." But they'd tried everything else and it had failed. Now was the time for creative solutions. And he'd already been invited to stay at the colony. Why not use that stroke of luck to their advantage?

Bob Forster, one of the two senior partners in the firm, finally decided to comment. "Just how are you going to carry off this charade? You're not a writer."

"That's a minor detail," Tristan said. "I'm sure I'll have to provide some type of work at some point, but I'll do my best to delay that. My sole focus will be to spend time with the Pigglestone sisters and try to get to know them better. If I can get them to trust me, they may consider an offer from us."

Reggie Dunlap, the other half of Forster and Dunlap, chuckled softly. "I'll say this. It's a damn creative approach to our problem. You're nothing if not charming, Quinn. I'll give you that. So, how long do you think it will take before we have an answer?"

"That depends," Tristan said.

"On what?" Forster asked.

"On how long I can pretend to be Quinn James. And how long it takes for the sisters to trust me."

"What about Lily Harrison?" Forster asked. "She's the one who has the most influence on the old ladies. How are you going to deal with her?"

"I suspect she'll be the easiest," Tristan said. After all, he could already sense she was attracted to him. He wouldn't be surprised if she'd been the one to convince the sisters to offer him a spot at the colony.

"Still, she'll be the most suspicious. And I'm not satisfied that you've covered yourself on the writing angle. You need a manuscript."

Tristan's assistant, Melanie Parker, timidly raised her hand. Legal assistants usually didn't speak at partners' meetings, but this wasn't just any meeting. "Melanie?"

"I—I'd like to offer a suggestion," she said. "I do a little writing myself and I've been working on a novel for about a year now. It's a legal thriller with some romance thrown in. It's almost done. I could give it to Tristan to use as his own writing."

"That's very generous of you," Tristan said.

"Who knows," she said. "Maybe you'll be able to make a connection with a famous writer who'll help me get it published. At the worst, I could get some criticism or helpful notes."

Tristan didn't have the heart to tell her that the colony was made up of retirees and has-beens. He doubted there was anyone there who had any connections at all to publishing. But Melanie was a good person who was helping him out. If this plan worked, he'd find a way to make those connections for her. Tristan almost hoped that the book was bad, though. It would make Lily less suspicious.

"It's a good plan," Reggie said. He stood up, effectively calling an end to the meeting. "You've got a month, Quinn. You get the job done properly, you'll be up for junior partner."

Tristan stood as the partners left the conference room. When they were gone, he let out a tightly held breath. "Thank you," he said, smiling at Melanie as he flopped back down in his chair. "I think your suggestion sealed the deal."

"Maybe I shouldn't have brought it up," she said. "Now everyone will wonder if I have plans to be an author, instead of the best darn paralegal at Forster and Dunlap. Maybe it would be better if you told them all that my book is really, really bad."

Tristan gathered his papers and tossed them into his briefcase. "I doubt it's bad," he said. "I think you'd make a great author." He paused and snapped his briefcase shut. "Don't you ever wonder what you're really supposed to be doing in this world? I mean, maybe you were meant to be a writer and not a paralegal."

"I'd like to think so," Melanie said. "When you read my book, will you promise to give me your honest opinion?"

Tristan met her gaze and saw a vulnerability there that he'd only seen on a few prior occasions. He'd come to depend on Melanie over the three years they'd worked together. In truth, he felt somewhat protective of her, almost as if she were his little sister. Her dark hair was always pulled back in a haphazard bun and her horn-rimmed glasses sat on her nose at a perpetually crooked angle. She also seemed to prefer frumpy business suits that could only be described as unflattering.

There were times when he'd caught her looking at him with an odd expression on her face, and he wondered if she might harbor some unrequited feelings for him. But then she'd return to business as usual and he'd realize that there was at least one woman in the world who was immune to his charm.

"So, why don't we get a copy of your manuscript and let's talk about it."

"Really? I haven't told anyone that I've been writing. You'll be the first to read it."

"What's the title?"

"*Legal Tender*," she said.

"Nice title."

2

Lily sat on the front steps of her cottage, her arms wrapped around her knees and her gaze fixed on the drive leading out to the main road. It was 3 p.m. and she had been waiting for Quinn's arrival since nine that morning.

"Get a grip," she muttered to herself. Why not just go about her business as if this were just any other day? Today, she'd already walked down to the bathhouse and taken a shower. Then she'd sat on the end of the dock and combed through her hair before heading to the dining hall for breakfast. Lunch was followed by a short trip to her studio before she decided to give up entirely and focus her attention on the road.

What if he decided not to return? If her suspicions were correct and he was a lawyer pretending to be a writer, then he'd have every reason not to come back. His lies could easily be exposed, especially if he couldn't produce a manuscript.

"Hey, Lily. That's a pretty dress. Are you going into town?"

She forced a smile as Bernie Wilson shuffled up. Bernie was the only working author that lived at the colony, and at forty-five, he was also the only man even remotely close to her own age. He'd somehow taken this simple fact and twisted it into a belief that they were destined to be together.

Bernie wrote science fiction and made a decent living with his craft. He certainly didn't need to live at the colony, but he'd been spending his summers on Fence Lake for the past eight years and in that time, had become their most successful resident.

"I heard someone new is moving in," he mumbled, pushing his glasses up on his nose.

Lily nodded. "Yes. He'll be arriving later today, I think."

"Where's he going to stay?"

"There's an extra bedroom in Finch's cabin. He'll stay there until we can get one of the cabins on the peninsula cleaned up for him."

"I spotted a yellow-bellied sapsucker today," Bernie said. "Right over there, on the point."

"Yeah, they've been around," Lily said. She stood up and brushed the dust from the front of her dress. "I'll see you later, Bernie."

"Are you coming to critique group tonight?"

"No, I don't have anything to read. And Violet is doing some scenes from Othello with Billy tonight. She's probably going to want my help setting up the stage."

"Sure. No problem. Maybe next week." He turned to walk away, then stopped. "You write really nice poetry," Bernie said.

Lily smiled. "Thanks, Bernie. I should probably get to work on my painting. Bye."

She hurried off in the direction of the tree house studios, the sound of harp music drifting on the humid morning air. Evaleen Deschanter, a folksinger, sat on the porch of her cabin, plucking on the harp strings as she sang a tragic ballad of ill-fated lovers.

"Hi, Lily," Evaleen said, smiling slyly as she came closer. "I hear we're getting a new member of the colony today. Violet says he's quite a handsome young man. I can hardly wait to meet him."

Gossip raced around the colony like wildfire in a dry field. Lily usually barely paid attention to it, but now some of the attention seemed to have turned toward her. This man could possibly be the enemy and everyone was delighted to let him in the gate.

Lily shook her head. "He's very charming. I expect he'll be very popular with the ladies."

There were twenty-one artists who spent part or all of the summer at the colony. Fourteen of them were women and Lily was the only one who hadn't yet celebrated her sixty-seventh birthday. The seven men were all over seventy, with the exception of Bernie, who was in his mid-forties. Lily had accepted the fact that she was spending her days and nights in a veritable retirement community. But now that was all about to change.

She passed three more artists and they offered her the same pleasant greeting and hopeful wishes. By the time she climbed the narrow steps up to her studio and dropped the trapdoor on the tree house, she could barely hold her temper in check.

The studios had all been built on stilts overlooking the lake. Of all the spots in the colony, her studio was where she felt most herself. Screened on four sides, it caught the summer breeze and it was just cozy enough to hold everything she needed for her painting. The trees blocked views of the other studios, so privacy was never an issue. She could cry, she could sing, she could tear off all her clothes and dance around and no one could see.

Lily raised the shutters to let in the light. Afternoon sun filtered in through the leaves on the trees, and she found a spot of light perfect for her work. She grabbed an abstract painting she'd recently begun and set it on an easel. Then she pulled up a stool and sat down, studying the painting for a long moment.

She'd never been a very good judge of her own work, but this painting seemed to be something special, a step ahead for her.

There had been moments in the past few years when she'd felt this way, as if she'd opened a door or discovered a new window and found something wonderful inside. But it hadn't been often, and she usually found herself in front of a blank or disappointing canvas wondering what she was doing with her life.

Lily was lucky that she had money from her family to support her. Still, she wanted to believe that her work was headed somewhere. Maybe when this piece was done she'd finally feel she was a true artist.

It was easy to lose herself in her work, and before she knew it, an hour had passed. Her hands were covered with paint and there were rags that she'd used to wipe her brushes tossed about the floor. The painting now looked more focused, a new layer of color adding a deeper meaning. But she couldn't help noticing that the color was very similar to that of Quinn James's hair...

The sound of a bell ringing caught her attention and she stood up. Without telephones or a public address system, the camp relied on a single brass bell, mounted next to the door of the dining hall, to call the residents for a meal or to assemble for a meeting. There was only one reason to ring it at this time of the day. Their new guest had arrived!

Her heart skipped a beat and Lily felt a wild sense of anticipation. She hadn't been able to put Quinn out of her head since the moment he had left the day before. Now that he was here, she had a better chance of figuring him out. Was he a wolf dressed in writer's clothing? Or was he just a charming guy who enjoyed flirting with a single woman?

Until she knew exactly who he was and what he wanted, she reminded herself to maintain her distance. But she would at least greet him along with the others. She climbed down the stairs and ran along the soft dirt path that led back to the main lodge.

When she reached the clearing, she noticed a large crowd had already gathered. Lily made a quick count and smiled to herself when the number matched the total number at camp. "I guess we're all excited," she murmured.

Lily slowly approached the group, her gaze on the man removing his bags from the trunk of his sports car. He was dressed differently today. His dress shirt and tie had been discarded in favor of relaxed shorts and a faded T-shirt. Sunglasses still hid his eyes and his thick, dark hair was covered by a baseball cap.

She moved to stand beside Aunt Violet, knowing that the eldest sister would be the one to make the official welcome. And as she had so many times over the years, Violet made a lovely little speech celebrating the event and introducing Quinn James to the entire group. After a quick round of applause and individual introductions, the group wandered off and Quinn was left with just three others—Violet, Lily and Finch.

Lily held out her hand. "It's good to have you here, Quinn. I hope you enjoy your stay."

"Thanks, Lily."

A long silence descended between them and Lily continued to smile, waiting for Violet to chime in.

When she didn't, Lily said, "I need to get back to my work." She held up her paint-stained fingers. "I'm having a—a breakthrough. Very exciting. Perhaps I'll see you this evening?"

"I was hoping that you would show Mr. James around the colony," Violet said.

"I thought Finch did that yesterday," Lily said.

"I only gave him a very brief tour," Finch explained.

"And I've asked Mr. Finch to drive me into town to pick up a few things for tonight's performance, haven't I, Mr. Finch?"

The elderly man looked back and forth between the

two women, then finally nodded. "Yes, you have, Miss Violet, you certainly have. And yesterday I just gave Mr. James a quick tour. My cabin, the dining hall. There's much more for you to show him, Lily. I'll just carry Mr. Quinn's bags up to the cabin and then fetch the car."

"Don't worry," Quinn said. "I can take care of that."

Lily's heart was beating so hard she was certain everyone around her could hear it. She swallowed hard. "Fine, let's go, then." Lily turned to Quinn. "Ready?"

"Lead on," he said.

She picked up a pair of his smaller bags, then pointed in the direction of Finch's cabin. "This way."

As they walked, Lily tried to come up with something to say to him, but her mind was racing with thoughts of their first encounter and the attraction that had pulsed between them. "I hope you're ready to live in rather primitive conditions," she said. "There's a sink in each cabin, but no en suite plumbing. For that, you have to go to the shower house just down the hill. Or pee in the woods, which most of the men do."

"That doesn't sound so bad."

"There are screens on all the windows, but you'll need to lower the shutters to keep the rain out. Some of the evenings can be chilly, so I hope you brought some heavy blankets."

"I thought I'd go into town and buy whatever I needed," he said. "Heavy blankets. I'll put that on my list."

When they reached the cabin, Lily pulled the door open, and stepped back to let him inside. The interior was cozy, the walls lined with windows and shabby furniture scattered about. Finch worked at a small desk by the window that he'd covered with papers and books. "You can take the empty bedroom. And we'll find you another spot to work. One of the tree house studios is empty."

"Tree house? That sounds like fun," he said, setting the bags down on the floor.

"They're not really tree houses, but…well, you'll see." She smoothed her hands over the front of her dress. "Is there somewhere else you'd like me to take you? I'm not sure how much Finch showed you yesterday."

"You combed your hair," he murmured. Quinn took a step toward her.

Lily quickly stepped back, her hand fluttering to her neck before she ran her fingers through the thick waves. "No. I—I mean, yes. I don't always look like a—a wreck."

He took another step, but this time, Lily held her ground. "I like your hair all messed up," he said. Quinn took another step. He was close enough to reach out and touch a strand of hair that had curled on her temple. With gentle fingers, he tucked the curl behind her ear.

"It gets a little wild with the humidity," she murmured.

Lily held her breath as he closed the last bit of distance between them. His gaze was fixed on hers and she knew he was about to kiss her. Every instinct told her to run away, to escape before he lured her into his trap. But she couldn't contain her curiosity. It was just a kiss. And though she wasn't sure who he was, Lily certainly knew who she was—and who she wasn't.

She wasn't the kind of girl who could be swept away by a stranger who might or might not be her enemy. She wasn't the kind of girl who would let a simple kiss alter her judgement. She wasn't—

His hands snaked around her waist and he pulled her against him. A few seconds later, his mouth came down on hers and she was drawn into a deep abyss of sensation. Her body felt weightless, her knees like they were ready to collapse. And when they did, she sank against the hard muscle and bone of his chest.

He drew back, his eyes scanning her face, trying to gauge her reaction. But Lily was still reeling from the aftereffects of the experience.

"I've been thinking about doing that since we met yesterday."

"You have?" Her voice was breathless and she felt her cheeks warm. Fantasies of being seduced by him had been teasing her for the past twenty-four hours. But now that the reality was looking down at her with a tempting smile, Lily realized that she was in danger of getting in over her head.

"I should go," she murmured. "And let you get settled."

"Would you like to come into town with me?"

Lily shook her head. "No, I need to paint. You know how it is. When things are going well you don't want to stop."

He bent closer and dropped another kiss on her lips.

"Seemed things were going very well there just a few minutes ago."

Lily nodded. "Don't forget to buy food in town. We all make our own meals except for Wednesday nights and Sunday afternoons. Then we have a potluck and everyone is assigned a dish. And please don't ever kiss me again."

With that, Lily turned and hurried to the door. Such strange sensations were running through her body, she thought as she pulled the screen door open. The temptation to stay and see what else might happen was nearly overwhelming her common sense!

She ran down the path toward her studio, but instead of climbing the steps to the loft, she turned toward the beach. Lily reached for the hem of her dress and pulled it over her head, discarding it on the small strip of sand at the water's edge.

As she waded into the lake, the cool water hit her naked body and immediately calmed her nerves and erased all those unfamiliar sensations that his kiss had caused. She kicked her feet, diving down until she stroked the sandy bottom, then she popped up to the surface and raked her hair back as she stood.

This was what she'd have to do if she expected to cool her libido and survive the summer. She'd have to take up residence in the middle of Fence Lake.

TRISTAN STOOD AT the edge of the path, his gaze fixed on the naked woman splashing in the lake. Apparently, Lily wasn't aware of his presence and he felt a bit guilty for watching her. But she seemed to live her life by a different set of rules—rules that didn't include underwear…or inhibitions…or the ability to keep from saying whatever popped into her mind.

He'd never been quite so intrigued by a woman, and his lawyerly instincts wanted to delve deeper, to find out what she was all about. He'd always been adept at reading women, at navigating past what they wanted him to think in order to get to the truth. Most of the women he'd known were just illusions, a pretty web of carefully crafted lies and wishful fabrications sprinkled with an undercurrent of cool and calculating greed. Once he'd stripped away the pretty wrappings, he lost interest.

But with Lily, there were no wrappings. What she presented to the world was pure and true and he found that endlessly intriguing. She hadn't tried to turn herself into every male's fantasy. She wore no makeup, her hair wasn't straightened or teased or sprayed, and from what he could tell, she hadn't had a single surgical enhancement.

Instead, her skin was kissed a golden brown by the sun and her nose sprinkled with freckles. Her hairdresser was whatever breeze blew by that day and she chose her fashion not to flatter, but to provide the greatest amount of comfort.

His mind wandered back to the kiss they'd shared. When he kissed a woman, it was usually a prelude to seduction. But with Lily it had been more about curiosity than anything else. She had tried to create distance between them, but he sensed that there was more to her feelings than she revealed. It wasn't just a simple flirtation that could be fed by a kiss or a caress. She was holding something back.

A glint of light flashed in the woods, drawing Tristan's attention away from Lily. Through the brush, he saw the figure of a man, hunched down, binoculars trained on her as she swam.

Cursing softly, Tristan emerged from the bushes and started toward the voyeur. But the guy caught sight of him and disappeared into the woods. Tristan didn't pursue him. It was obviously someone from the colony, and it wouldn't take Tristan long to figure out who.

As he walked to the shore, he snatched up her discarded dress, then whistled through his teeth. Lily immediately stood to face him, her naked breasts exposed and gleaming in the morning light. Tristan expected her to sink back down into the water, but she didn't. Instead, she tipped her chin up and stared at him with defiance in her eyes.

"What do you want?"

"I want you to come out of the water and put your clothes on," he said.

She dipped down and then rose again, tipping her chin up as she stood and smoothing her hair back. "I want to swim," she said. "I need the exercise."

"You need to put your clothes on before anyone else comes looking. I just chased off one Peeping Tom, I don't want to have to chase off any more."

"Who appointed you my protector?"

"You apparently require one," Tristan said. "So I guess I'm your guy."

With a curse, she started toward him. As her naked body began to emerge from the water, Tristan held out her dress and angled his gaze away.

"What's wrong with you?" she muttered. "Are you going to melt if you catch a glimpse of a naked woman?"

"No," he said. "I just thought you'd enjoy your privacy."

"It's just a naked body," she said. "The same as any other naked body. I have all the proper parts, so there's nothing of interest to see." Lily snatched the dress from his hand, but when he finally turned, she hadn't bothered to put it on.

With a curse more vivid than hers, Tristan grabbed the dress, shook it out and then held it over her head. He tried to keep from looking as she raised her arms, but the sight was impossible to ignore. A surge of desire washed over him and he fought the temptation to toss the dress aside and strip off his own clothes.

He could almost feel her naked body against his, skin to skin, the soft flesh of her breasts pressed to his chest. His fingers twitched as he imagined running his hands along her torso, smoothing his palms over her hips and backside.

"Are you sure you're a writer?" she muttered, the dress falling over her until her damp body was once again covered.

Tristan sucked in a sharp breath. Had he given himself away already? "Why?"

"Most of the writers I've known haven't been prudes."

"Like I said, there was a guy watching you from the shore. He had binoculars. Who can say what his intentions were?"

"That was Bernie."

"Bernie, the science fiction guy? The one I met this morning."

Lily leaned over and twisted the water from her dripping hair. "Yes, Bernie. He's harmless."

"You don't mind that he watches you?"

"He hasn't seen many naked women in his life. He's kind of shy and I suppose he's curious."

Tristan laughed. "So you're doing him a public service by letting him gawk?"

She shrugged, droplets of water glinting off her dark lashes. "I can't search the woods every time I want to go for a swim." Lily started toward the path, her bare feet kicking up sand and dirt until they were covered in both.

Tristan strode after her. "Why did you run away after I kissed you?"

"Because unlike Bernie, you're not harmless. In fact, I think you're a very dangerous man, Mr. Quinn James…if that is your real name."

Tristan bit back a curse. It was clear she was suspicious of him. But how deep did that go? Was it just his romantic interest that made her wary? Or did she suspect the level of his deception? "Lots of writers use pen names," he said.

"Published writers," she countered. "*Is* Quinn your real name?"

"It is," Tristan lied. He knew what she meant and

he also knew he was twisting the truth to suit his own purposes. But in the end, he could freely admit that Quinn was his real name.

"And why did you kiss me? Would you like to try the truth on *that* question?"

Tristan grabbed her hand and pulled her to a stop, spinning her around to face him. He wasn't sure he could put an answer into words. Right now, standing here with her just inches away in a dress that clung to her wet body, he had an undeniable need to draw her into his arms and put his mouth to hers once again. But that would hardly put her suspicions to rest.

"It seemed like the only thing to do," Tristan said in a soft voice. "I couldn't help myself." He shook his head. "Do you have any idea how beautiful you are? Do you understand what that kind of beauty does to a man?"

Lily stared at him for a long moment, then laughed. It wasn't a nervous laugh or even a sarcastic laugh. She clearly considered his statement ridiculous.

"'Beauty is not found in the face. It's a light in the heart.'"

"Who told you that?"

"My aunts. It's from the poet Kahlil Gibran. My aunts raised me to believe that true beauty was found inside me and had nothing to do with my outside appearance."

"Well, this might shock you, but they were wrong. You're beautiful on the outside, too, Lily, and it's about time someone told you that."

"I'll alert the media," she muttered. "News flash—

another beautiful woman in the world. I'm sure they'll want to rush right over and get the story."

"Hasn't anyone ever told you how beautiful you are? Your mother or father?"

"I didn't spend a lot of time with my parents. During the school year, they sent me to a very strict Catholic boarding school where mirrors and all beauty products were banned and conformity was enforced. And in the summer, I lived here with my aunts, where I was encouraged to let my spirit run free."

"Wow," Tristan replied. "That must have been some childhood."

"Not all of us were blessed with perfect parents. Mine didn't have *children*, they produced *heirs*."

"My parents weren't Ward and June Cleaver, either."

Lily frowned. "Who are Ward and June Cleaver?"

"From *Leave It To Beaver*. Nick at Nite? It's an old television show."

"I think I saw that once."

"Once?"

"Or twice. We didn't have American television at boarding school. And the aunts never allowed a television here in the colony. I don't remember beavers in the show."

"No, that was the name of their son," Tristan explained.

"They named their son Beaver? That's just cruel. I hope he changed it when he got older. Although I suppose some might not mind it. Beavers are very intelligent and industrious animals. Finch's spirit animal is a beaver. Mine is a wren. I suspect yours is probably a wolf."

She started along the path again, but this time, Tristan didn't let go of her hand. "I'm beginning to think you and I must have been born on different planets."

"Are your parents aliens?"

This made Tristan laugh. "My father was."

"Tell me about them," she said. "They couldn't have been worse than mine."

"That's a story for a different day," Tristan said.

They had reached a small building, set on stilts, and Lily stopped. "This is my studio," she said.

"Are you going to show it to me? I'd like to see your work."

Lily hesitated, and for an instant, Tristan thought he might have won her over. But she stymied him again. "That will also have to be for a different day," she said.

It was very clear from the look on her face that this was meant to be "goodbye," but Tristan wasn't ready to let her go. He needed some excuse to see her again. It unsettled him that he hadn't quite gained her trust. "Do you have any plans for dinner tonight? We could drive into town and find a place."

"I usually eat here," she said.

"But you're a nonconformist. Take a risk and have dinner with me."

"I know we're the only two people of our age here at the colony. And it's only natural that we should hang around together. But I think it would be best if we just tried to be friends. We can sit together at the performance tonight, though, and I'll treat you to a lemon-ade."

Shakespeare and lemonade? Tristan couldn't re-member the last time he'd had such a chaste date. His usual dating itinerary consisted of drinks followed by no-strings sex. Or dinner followed by no-strings sex. Occasionally, lunch followed by— Tristan stopped himself. He suspected that he wouldn't be adding *Othello* and sex to the list later that night.

"*Othello* would be interesting," he said. "I don't think I've ever seen it."

"I assure you, it will be much better entertainment than that Beaver show you watch."

"It's a date," he said, leaning in to steal one last kiss.

But Lily caught him before his lips met hers, press-ing her finger against his mouth. "It's Shakespearean drama. And that's all." She started up the stairs. "Oh, and if nudity is a problem for you, then you should probably stay locked in your cabin on Saturday nights after sunset. That's when everyone goes for a skinny-dip. It's a tradition when the weather is still warm."

"Everyone?"

"Well, the older folks. I usually leave them to their fun. It can turn into a bit of an orgy. Of course, I'm sure the ladies would be thrilled if you joined in."

Tristan gasped. "You don't mean that literally, do you?"

"There's a lot of sex that goes on here," she said. "And *none* of it has to do with me." With that, she spun and crawled up the steep stairs. "I know you're look-ing up my skirt," she said. "Stop it."

Tristan turned away and started down the path toward his cabin, confused. He'd had a lot of experience with women, enjoyed a lot of different relationships. But what was going on with Lily was beyond his experience. One moment they seemed like intimate friends and the next, they were snapping and sniping at each other and she was pushing him away. It was the damnedest thing, Tristan mused. And he was determined to figure it all out before it drove them both over the edge.

THE LATE AUGUST sun had disappeared below the horizon by the time everyone started to gather for what Violet was calling a *"petit divertissement."* Over the course of the summer and the early fall, the inhabitants of the Fence Lake artists' colony produced all sorts of entertainments, from musical revues to modern dance spectacles to productions of classic plays.

For tonight's performance, Lily played her part by standing at the door and passing out programs she had designed at Violet's behest.

Tonight, Billy Chadwick-Farnsworth, an elderly British playwright and sometime actor, had planned to stage scenes and soliloquies from Shakespeare's *Othello.* Billy had been coming to Fence Lake for as long as Lily could remember. During the winter months, he returned to England to live with his daughter in Bath. But this year, there was gossip around the camp that he might decide to stay and pursue a newfound romance with Violet.

Little romances seemed to crop up every summer.

Usually they were short-lived, and Lily didn't expect this one would last long. Violet, though passionate about love, was far too independent to handle living with a man for more than a few weeks. A month had been the longest Lily could remember her staying with a man, and that had been with a sculptor who did all the cooking and cleaning.

Lily smiled to herself as she remembered her first romance at the camp. A handsome young photographer had wandered in one day, looking for a place to stay as he traveled across the country. She'd been nineteen. The passion between them had been instant. He'd stayed for a month before walking out of her life forever.

The thought of him brought a flood of bittersweet memories, but she had never regretted the affair. When she had passion in her life, her artistic talents came alive. Her emotions were the fuel that produced stunning work that she never seemed to be able to replicate on her own.

Could she allow herself the same indulgence with Quinn? She was older and wiser now. As she approached her twenty-eighth birthday, she knew that the time for passionate affairs was beginning to end. Her aunts had always told her that passions waned as wisdom grew. The older one became, the more difficult it was to forget the past and trust in love.

What if Quinn James was her last chance to produce truly great art? Each of her aunts had experienced that kind of love and spoke fondly of the men who had served as their muses.

Her last lover had been a Frenchman, two years ago. The affair had fueled an intense period of work. It had been a memorable summer, but she'd never completely surrendered her heart to him. Even as he'd walked out of camp, she'd known that another man would appear someday.

What if Quinn was that man? The one who would finally allow her to call herself a true artist? Then again, she'd never had to worry that any of her previous lovers were actually snakes in the grass. Could she be Quinn's lover without trusting him?

"What are you frowning about?"

He stood behind her and Lily felt his hands slip around her waist.

"Nothing," she lied, turning to face him. "What are you smiling about?"

"I'm happy to see you again. I've spent all evening looking forward to this."

Lily pressed a program into his chest, pushing him away. "I thought you came here to work. If you spend your time thinking about me, how are you going to get anything done?"

"Maybe you inspire me," he said. "Maybe you're my muse?"

"That line has been used around this place far too often. More like I'm your amusement."

"You are amusing, Lily. I have to admit that. So if you're my amusement, what am I to you?"

"I don't know. Perhaps you're my Kryptonite."

Quinn frowned. "You're familiar with Kryptonite, but you don't recognize the Cleavers?"

"I read a lot of comic books when I was younger. And we've had several graphic novelists here in camp." She saw Bernie approach and Lily held out a program to him.

"I saved a seat for you in the front row," Bernie said. "When you're finished with the programs you can sit there."

"Thank you, Bernie," she began.

"Thank you, Bernie," Quinn interrupted, "but she's going to sit with me. I'm surprised you'd choose the first row. Aren't you the kind of guy who likes to observe from a distance?"

Bernie's face turned red and he hurried back to his seat.

"That wasn't very nice," Lily said. "He's not a bad guy. And I'm sure there's a woman out there for him. It's just not me."

"Exactly. So there's no reason for him to watch you swimming in the lake, especially when you choose to do it naked."

"Oh, you've gone from Kryptonite to White Knight. How wonderful."

Violet appeared on the small stage and the house lights slowly dimmed. She wore a flowing dress made of iridescent ivory silk and chiffon with a beaded bodice. Her gray hair was loose and fell in waves down her back. A jeweled headband covered her forehead. She looked like something out of a Rudolph Valentino silent movie with her dark eyes and deep red lips.

"Come on," he whispered, taking Lily's hand and pulling her toward the door.

"I want to stay and watch," Lily protested.

"We'll be back before it's over," he assured her.

Lily refused to move until Billy launched into one of Othello's soliloquies. She glanced over at Quinn, knowing exactly what would happen when they were alone. He'd kiss her again…and again…and maybe again. And suddenly, it wouldn't be enough. She'd need more.

Lily groaned inwardly. She'd promised herself that she wouldn't surrender to him until she was sure he wasn't a secret enemy infiltrator. To do that, she had to get a look at his novel. "Let's go," she whispered.

They snuck out the back, running away from the light that spilled off the wide verandah on the low log building. When they reached the beach, he pulled her into his arms and kissed her. Lily's blood warmed and her heart began to race as her fingers tangled in his soft hair.

He wore a scent so tantalizing, she wanted to bury her face in the curve of his neck and inhale deeply. His mouth tasted of cinnamon. She experienced him with every sense she possessed.

He seemed to be enjoying the same experience. His fingertips skimmed over her body, splaying wide against the small of her back before circling her waist. His tongue delved deep and when he cupped her breast in his palm, Lily moaned softly.

"There's something I want," she murmured.

"Anything," he whispered, his voice low and husky, his breath warm against her throat.

"I want to read your novel."

Her request caught him by surprise and he frowned. "My novel? Now?"

"Yes. Do you have a copy?"

"Back in my cabin," he said.

"Let's go," she said, grabbing his hand and pulling him toward the path.

"It's five hundred pages long. You won't be able to read it in one night."

"Then I'll take it with me."

"I only brought one copy."

"We have a photocopier in the rec hall. I can make a bunch of copies."

"Wouldn't you rather go back and watch *Othello*?"

Lily stopped and faced him. What was that? Four excuses? Or was it five? "Is there some reason you don't want me to read your work?" He gave her an uneasy smile. He was hiding something and Lily intended to get to the bottom of it. "Is there even a novel?"

"Of course there is," Quinn said. "Why would you think there wasn't?"

"I'm not sure. But I have to wonder if you made it up. Just to get an invitation to the colony."

"So I could get to know you better?" Quinn nodded.

"Perhaps," she said. "What other possible reason could you have?"

"I guess I'll just have to prove it to you." This time, he grabbed her hand. Lily had trouble keeping up with his long stride and when they reached his cabin, she was out of breath.

Quinn opened the door and ushered her inside. The room was lit by an old stand lamp next to Finch's desk and another smaller lamp on a table at the end of the sofa. Neither one of the lamps provided enough light to read by. "There's better light in my bedroom," he said as if he could read her mind. "I bought a new lamp this afternoon. And my manuscript is in there."

Lily drew a deep breath and gathered her resolve. Just entering his bedroom would be fraught with peril, but she had to find out if he was a writer. If there was no book, it was proof that he had ulterior motives for being at the colony. If he was, then perhaps she could indulge in the kind of wild affair that she needed.

She slowly walked into the dark room. He came in behind her and she closed her eyes, waiting for him to touch her, to pull her into his arms and kiss her again. She'd come to crave that first rush of desire, that moment when she lost touch with reality and surrendered to his taste and his touch.

How easy it had been to accept this addiction. And like all addictions, she knew her need would only grow with time. Already, a simple kiss was no longer enough to satisfy her. Now she wanted his hands on her body or his body pressed against hers, or—

Lily sucked in a sharp breath as the light flipped on. He stood next to the bed, a sheaf of papers clutched in his hand. Slowly, he pulled back the mosquito netting that was strung around the bed. "Why don't you take this and get started. I'm going to walk back down and watch the show."

"You can stay," she said.

"That would be far too much temptation for me. I imagined quite a different scene when I invited you into my bed for the first time. I'll come and get you before the grand finale."

Lily took the manuscript from his outstretched hand. "All right. I'll see you in a bit."

"I hope you like it," he said.

Lily looked at him for a long moment. "What?"

He nodded toward the papers she held. "The novel. I hope you like it." With that, Quinn turned and left the bedroom.

Lily drew a deep breath as she stared down at the cover page. "*Legal Tender.*" There was no author name. She crawled onto the bed and pulled the mosquito net around her, then adjusted the two pillows. "Let's see what kind of writer you are, Mr. Quinn James."

From the very first line, the story captured her imagination. It began with a crime so cunning and complex that Lily immediately found herself invested in the victims. Strangely, it was a crime without a hint of violence. Instead, it tore apart the fabric of a dozen peoples' lives, putting them through a hell that they never could have anticipated.

The scenes were gripping and emotional, each one leading to the next so it was impossible to stop reading. Every chapter ended in an emotional or a physical cliffhanger, and each one built the conflicts to a crescendo.

Lily was stunned at how tight the writing was. His style was simple, yet vivid, tiny details adding to the narrative. Flowery prose was almost nonexistent. As a romance developed between the main characters—a female law student and a private detective—Lily was impressed by his handling of both characters' inner voices.

Often, it was easy to tell if a book was written by a male or a female, simply by the way they wrote about the opposite sex. But Quinn had a real knack for getting inside a woman's head and knowing how and what she thought.

Lily set down the manuscript. Maybe that was why he was so good at seducing her, she mused. Maybe he knew exactly what she was thinking when he kissed her or touched her. That would certainly answer a lot of the questions she had.

A cool breeze blew through the bedroom and Lily snuggled down in the bed, pulling the edge of the new down blanket over her and closing her eyes for a moment. So, Quinn really was a writer and not some mysterious interloper.

A tiny shiver skittered down her spine and Lily groaned softly. So that meant she could cast aside the last of her doubts about him and accept his advances. But some instinct, deep inside her, was still sounding a warning bell, a noise that was getting ever louder since the moment they'd met.

Quinn was the kind of man who'd be dangerous to a woman's mind and her heart. Any short-term love affair required one thing—a man that could be both memorable and forgettable at the same time. Though Lily suspected that making love to Quinn would be incredible, she also suspected he might ruin her for any other man who might come down the road in the future.

And she couldn't have that. He could be good, great

even. But he couldn't be the best ever. If he was, then it would be over for her. Her creative juices would die with her love life. At nearly twenty-eight she'd have met, loved and lost that one man. And like her aunts, she'd live off that memory for the rest of her life.

Lily wasn't ready to leave that part of her life behind. Not until she'd created a masterpiece, at least! "Maybe he isn't that good," she whispered, pulling the down blanket up around her nose. Was there a choice between flirtatious romance and full-on seduction? Of course there was. And though grown adults usually skipped right to the latter, she was certainly able to control the pace of their relationship...

3

TRISTAN STOOD AT the rear of the theater, watching as the last part of the night's production began. The heat from the old lights had made the interior almost unbearable, and many of the audience had moved to stand near the screened windows and the double door at the rear.

He'd promised to fetch Lily for the ending, but he'd decided against it, knowing it might be difficult to lure her back to the cabin once she left. Besides, this production was like no other *Othello* he'd ever imagined.

Though he didn't know much Shakespeare, he was sure it wasn't supposed to be like this. Billy was performing his role quite admirably as he swept around the stage in a long robe with a tattered fur collar, his voice booming through the tiny theater.

Desdemona was another story altogether. As far as he could tell, the scene they were performing was the murder scene, when Othello drags Desdemona from her bed and smothers her with a pillow. However, Violet's Desdemona was dancing around the room when

Othello arrived and every one of her lines was also interpreted in a modern dance. Tristan felt like he was watching two separate productions mashed up into one.

He leaned over to Raymond Finch, who stood beside him. "Is it just me, or is this a bit...odd?"

"Odd might be a kind description," Finch said, his gaze fixed on Violet. "I think it's more bizarre than odd. But most of the colony's productions wander well outside the proverbial box." He glanced over at Tristan. "By the way, I've been asked to personally invite you to the writers' critique group. We're all quite anxious to read your work. We meet tomorrow morning at 10 a.m. in the gazebo. Bring a chapter of your manuscript to read. And another section to pass around for next time."

"I hadn't really planned to participate in—"

"Of course you'll participate. All the writers do. The group can offer many valuable insights. And that's why you're here, isn't it? To make your writing better?"

Tristan wondered how the critique group would feel if they learned the real reason he'd come. The offer to the three sisters was locked in his briefcase, which was itself secured in the trunk of his car. He had professional responsibilities, yet he'd let his fascination with Lily Harrison distract him from his job.

He might be able to convince himself that the attraction they felt couldn't be denied. But to allay her suspicions, he'd only have to keep lying to her about his identity and his motives. And he wasn't sure how much longer he could do that. But if she knew who he really was, then Lily would want nothing to do with him.

"How the hell did I get myself into this?" he muttered.

"What's that?" Finch whispered.

"Nothing," Tristan said.

Finch motioned him to the door, then stepped out onto the wide porch. He walked over to a pair of Adirondack chairs and sank down into one of them. Then he reached into his jacket and pulled out a small flask, opening it to take a swig.

"What sort of novel have you written?" Finch asked, holding out the flask to Tristan.

"It's a legal thriller," Tristan said, "with a bit of a romance thrown in." He took the flask and tipped it back, taking a long drink of the whiskey inside.

"Hmm. I wrote crime novels in my day. Now I'm working on my memoirs. In the fifties and sixties, you'd be run out of publishing on a rail if you included a romance in a crime novel. Men didn't want to read about love. And women didn't read crime novels. And you'd rarely find a legal novel. Lawyers weren't the heroes. Hard-boiled private investigators were. Times have changed, I guess."

"Lily told me that Bernie writes science fiction,"

"Yes," Finch said, nodding. "He's quite a good writer. I don't know why he comes back here every summer. I suspect it's because he has a thing for Lily." Finch frowned. "Where is Lily, by the way? I didn't see her inside."

"She's up at our cabin, reading my novel. She insisted I show it to her. I couldn't say no."

"I understand. A rare beauty like that should never

be refused anything she might want. I suppose you'll want me to find another place to sleep tonight."

"No," Tristan said. "Of course not. I expect she'll go home once I get back. I don't have any plans to— well, that's a pretty serious move after only meeting her yesterday."

Finch shrugged. "You're talking to a guy who lived through the sixties. Everyone around here is pretty much into free love."

"It's been my experience that love is never free," Tristan said.

"You just came of age in the wrong generation," Finch said. "You ought to try it. You might enjoy it."

"Do you think that's how Lily feels?"

"You'd have to ask her. I'm sure she would tell you *exactly* how she feels. Lily isn't one to keep her emotions to herself."

"Maybe I will," Tristan said. He heard clapping from inside the theater. "It sounds like they're done. I better go up and get her. I'll see you later."

"And if I don't see you later, will you be at critique group tomorrow morning?"

"I will," Tristan said as he jogged down the porch steps.

He hurried back to the cabin, suddenly worried about what Lily had thought of the manuscript. If he couldn't pull this off with her, then he'd never make it through the critique group. Although tomorrow he'd only be expected to give them a small number of pages. He'd need to study them carefully, though, so he could talk knowledgeably about his own work.

He pulled his cell phone out of his pocket and looked at it. It was only half past ten. Maybe he ought to call Melanie and get some good tips from her. In truth, he'd assumed it would be easy to pretend to be a writer. But now that he was going to be put the test, he realized that it would be as difficult as Lily pretending to be a lawyer.

He quietly opened the screen door and stepped inside. The light was still on in his bedroom. He kicked off his flip-flops and walked across the rough plank floor to the bedroom door.

Tristan smiled as he took a step toward the bed. She was wrapped in his new down blanket around her body and was sound asleep, the manuscript lying in the curve of her body, a sheaf of pages still clutched in her hand. He reached for the dimmer on the bedside lamp and brought the light down, leaving just enough of a glow for him to distinguish her pretty features in the dark.

Tristan carefully drew the netting back and retrieved the manuscript, then set it on the bedside table. Circling to the other side of the bed, he parted the mosquito net and crawled in beside her, slowly sinking down into the mattress. When he was stretched out beside her, Tristan wrapped his arm around her waist and gently pulled her back into the warmth of his body.

She moaned softly and snuggled against him. He wanted to turn her in his arms and kiss her awake and then see where the night went from there. But Tristan knew where that would lead, and he wasn't sure he was ready to take that step with Lily with so many lies between them.

He'd never had any hesitation in the past when it came to sex, but then he'd never been tangled in such a crazy web of deception. He realized he couldn't go any further with Lily until she knew the truth about him. Only then could she make a choice.

That left him with two options. He could put her off, keeping the relationship flirtatious but not sexual. Or he could take his offer to the sisters before the end of the week and see what happened once Lily knew the whole truth.

When he'd first met her, he hadn't really thought of the consequences of sleeping with her. But now that he'd spent an entire day in her presence, he realized that there was something very unusual about Lily. Instead of wanting to take advantage of her, Tristan wanted to protect her—especially from men like him. What kind of sense did that make?

He shifted and she moaned again, then turned in his arms and opened her eyes. As she rubbed her eyes, he saw that it took Lily a moment to figure out where she was. He watched the confusion fade from her expression, then he smiled. "Go back to sleep," he whispered.

"Is it over? Did I miss the big finale?"

"Yeah. It was really good. Your aunt was amazing. The way she can still move is kind of unbelievable. I've never seen anything quite like that performance."

Lily smiled sleepily. "You'll be saying that a lot if you stay here long enough." She pushed up on her elbow and he reached out and brushed the hair out of her eyes. "I read your book," she said.

"I see that. You're a fast reader. You almost got to the end."

"I skipped ahead. I wanted to find out what happened with the hero and heroine." She paused. "I wanted to read the sex scene."

The sex scenes. Melanie had told him there were a few in the book. But when he'd read it, he'd skipped over those pages, hoping to get on with the plot. The sex scenes were one part of the book that he couldn't speak of with any authority at all.

"I'm really interested in what you thought of the chase scene," he said, trying to divert her. "It's so difficult to write high action like that." In fact, Tristan had found the chase scene to be the weakest part of the book.

She shrugged. "I skipped over that part. But I loved the sex scene. There was such a tenderness between the two of them," Lily continued. "I read it three times and I think it might be the best ever written."

"No," Tristan said, shaking his head. "It's rubbish."

Lily looked at him with a perplexed frown. "It's just that men and women think about sex in different ways."

"Not so different," he replied.

"Oh, really? Tell me, what goes through your mind when you're...a woman? Is sex for a female character emotional or just primal? Men don't really think when they're doing it, do they?"

Her questioning was making him very uneasy and Tristan knew if this discussion went on any longer, she'd have reason to be suspicious again. "Can we talk about this another time?" he asked. "I'd really like your opinions, but I'm tired and still processing that *Othello* I just saw and—"

"Did you enjoy it?" Lily asked.

"It was very...original."

Lily smiled. "I'm sure it was." She pushed the down blanket off her body. "I should go. It's late."

"You can stay," Tristan said. "I want you to."

"What about Finch?"

"We're just going to sleep," Tristan said. "That's it. And to make sure, we'll leave our clothes on."

"Are you sure?" Lily asked, her gaze dropping to his lips. "Not even a kiss or two?"

Tristan slipped his hand around her nape and pulled her into a long, sweet kiss. "Okay, one kiss. Or three or four." He paused. "It might be nice to take things slowly. We have plenty of time."

Lily's gaze moved back to his, and she stared at him for a long moment as if she were trying to discern the truth in his words. "Is it too much for you?"

"What?"

"The crazy. Some people...men...don't really understand all this. It scares them. It's...out there."

He chuckled softly. "You don't scare me," he said, pulling her back against his body. "Now close your eyes and go to sleep. We'll talk more in the morning."

As Tristan held her, he felt her body relax and her breathing grow slow and regular.

Tristan wasn't sure what had possessed him to ask her to sleep in the same bed with him. She made him do strange things, and that worried him.

Women were complicated enough. Navigating his

way through the emotional minefield of a relationship was hard enough without knowing where all the explosives were buried. He felt vulnerable.

Tristan closed his eyes and tried to follow her into sleep. He'd sworn long ago that he'd never let anyone make him vulnerable ever again. But now he was ready to ignore hard-won common sense for a woman he barely knew.

"Maybe I'm the one who's a little crazy," he murmured.

LILY LOVED THE hour before sunrise, when the quiet of the night woods gave way to the chirping and singing of the birds. During the summer months, the birds were her alarm clock. She smiled and rolled over in bed, then froze.

Quinn was lying on the bed beside her, his arms and legs twisted at odd angles. Sometime during the night, he'd kicked off his shoes and unbuttoned his shirt, but he was still dressed.

Lily peered beneath the down blanket and frowned. She was still dressed, as well. When was the last time she'd slept with anything on? She usually found it impossible to fall asleep if she had anything on her body. Carefully, she pushed the blanket aside and swung her legs over the edge of his bed.

The chilly morning air hit her skin. Rubbing her arms to ward off goose bumps, she stepped out of the mosquito netting. By the sound of the birds and the dark blue color of the sky, she guessed that it was just before sunrise, about 6:30 a.m.

September was only a few days away and with it would come chilly nights and shorter days. Lily always felt a bit melancholy when the season came to an end. Everyone, with the exception of the aunts, scattered to the winds, heading south to the warmth or to hometowns where children and grandchildren awaited their arrival.

She looked back at Quinn, carefully taking in the details of his handsome face. He'd leave, too, going home to wherever he came from. Usually when she met a man she fancied, she could see their whole relationship in front of her. But Lily wasn't sure where her attraction to Quinn might lead. She still sensed that there was something a bit dangerous about him. He had the capacity to make her fall hard and fast. And a fall like that could hurt for a very long time.

Lily usually spent late fall and Christmas with her parents in Minneapolis, but the fight over ownership of the colony had caused a serious fracture in her family, with Lily on the side of her aunts and everyone else on the side of greed.

This year, she'd hoped to go directly to Europe and the friends she had waiting there. But she suspected that as soon as she left, her parents would increase their pressure on the aunts, and the three sisters might not be strong enough to continue on their own.

The entire case hinged on her great-great-grandfather's decision to gift the lake and all the land around it to his three daughters. But over the years, the property had been listed as an asset of the family foundation, a trust that doled out regular payments to all members of the family, from her parents to the most distant of first cousins.

Lily stretched her arms over her head, sighing softly as she worked the kinks out of her shoulders and neck. A morning swim would be the perfect thing to wake her up and relax her at the same time. Quinn would probably be expected to attend the writing critique group. While he was busy with that, Lily hoped to gather her aunts together and go over the next step in their plan.

Until now they'd used a pair of local lawyers to fight the property dispute, but Lily suspected that it was going to take someone with far more talent than those two, whose experience didn't extend beyond real estate closings and easement disputes.

She stared down at the handsome man asleep in the bed. Lily had suspected that he was a lawyer when he'd first arrived. What if he was? She could always test him a bit. If she asked Quinn about their problems, he'd have some ideas or advice. If it was good advice, she might be able to trust him. Then again, if he was working for her family, he might give her bad advice. But at least she'd know the kind of man he was.

She made a mental note to ask him some questions when she saw him later in the day. There was a lot she didn't know about Quinn James. But Lily wondered if all the silly little details—his favorite color, the way he drank his coffee, the name of his cologne—really made a difference at all.

In a month, he'd be gone from her life. After that, those unimportant things would just fade from her memory until she could barely recall what he looked like. A shiver skittered down her spine as she realized the depth of the lie she'd just told herself.

She might be able to forget the name of his favorite cologne, but there were other things she'd always remember. The feel of his warm palm on her bare skin. The taste of his mouth and the softness of his lips as he kissed her. And the way he sighed softly whenever her pulled her into his arms, as if the simple action gave him complete bliss.

Lily smiled as she tiptoed out of the room. By the time she reached the beach, the sun was up. As she tugged her dress over her head, she tested the water with her toe. Against the cool morning air, the lake felt as warm as bathwater. Tossing her dress to the sand, she slowly waded in.

Her thoughts wandered back to the night before. She'd fallen asleep in his bed. For any other man, that would have been an open invitation to seduction. And yet, nothing had happened.

Had she misread his original attraction? Or had something changed over the course of the day? She rewound the events and went over them one at a time. There were moments when she'd shown her doubts or insecurities, but still, things had been moving so quickly.

Lily sank down into the water, her hair spreading out around her face. She closed her eyes and threw her arms out until she floated on the surface of the water, allowing her mind to wander. An image of Quinn drifted through her head.

The sound of splashing caught her attention and Lily floundered until she regained her footing. But the surface of the water was clear. Suddenly, Quinn popped up in front of her, water rushing over his dark hair as he stood.

"What are you doing out here?" she asked.

He casually swam a wide circle around her, never taking his eyes from her. "Why would you crawl out of a nice warm bed with me and jump into a cold lake? I had to figure that out." He grinned. "Plus, I felt compelled to protect you from Bernie's prying eyes."

"He's usually not up this early," Lily said.

"And hasn't anyone ever told you that you should always swim with a buddy?"

Lily shook her head. "You want to be my buddy now? One might suspect your interests go beyond mere friendship."

"My intentions are purely honorable," he said.

"That's a shame," she teased. "I expected more from you."

"Did you?" He reached out and grabbed her hand, lacing his fingers through hers. Then he slowly pulled her through the water until their naked bodies bumped against each other. She felt his other hand slip around her waist and his fingers spread across the small of her back.

"Are you really going to begrudge me my inhibitions, Lily? Not everyone can be as open-minded as you are. It's just going to take me a little more time."

"Why? What will time give you?"

He reached up and smoothed his fingers over her

forehead, brushing a damp strand of hair back into place. "I want to get to know you better. And I want you to know me a little better, too."

"I know all I need to know," she said. Her hand dipped below the water and her fingers brushed against his cock.

"No you don't," he said.

Lily gently wrapped her fingers around him and he immediately began to grow hard beneath her touch. "Can you deny that you want me?" she asked, confident in her power over him.

He chuckled softly. "I'm not even going to attempt to do that. But our obvious need for each other isn't the only consideration here. If you really wanted anonymous sex, you could have found that anywhere."

"Like I said, I know enough to make this more than anonymous. If we get more acquainted, it would only make things too complicated," Lily said. "I don't care what your favorite color is or—"

"Blue," he said.

"Or what side of the bed you sleep on."

"Right down the middle," he said. "And I take my coffee black and I open my presents on Christmas Eve, not Christmas Day."

"For someone who enjoys no-strings relationships, there's too many strings right there. I don't need to know your favorite color, because I'm never going to buy you a shirt. I don't care where you like to sleep on the bed. If I'm in your bed, you'll have to move. I won't be serving you coffee, and we definitely won't be spending Christmas together."

"Well, I guess I'm just a little different," he said. "When I'm kissing you, I want you to know exactly who it is making you feel the way you feel."

He suddenly pushed away from her, swimming on his back. Her gaze fell on his shaft as it broke the surface of the water and a shiver raced through her at the power her touch had on his body. He was hard and ready and yet he still couldn't be convinced.

Lily cursed softly. If he was going to play these silly games, then she could participate, as well. She headed for shallow water and when her feet were beneath her, she walked toward the shore until the water had receded to her knees. Then she turned to face him.

Lily was well aware the effect her naked body would have on him, and she was delighted to see she hadn't overestimated her sexual powers. She smoothed her hands over her wet hair, then let her palms drift down her to breasts. "Do you really think there's anything more than this that you need to know?" she called.

He walked up to her, his pace slow and almost predatory. Lily tried to relax. But her heart pounded in her chest and her breathing came in short gasps. In less than a heartbeat, Quinn pulled her into his arms and they tumbled into the water, their mouths melded together.

He held tight as the kiss spun out, their limbs tangling. When they finally stood again, her legs were hitched up on his hips and the tip of his shaft teased at the opening between her legs. She closed her eyes and slowly leaned back, but Quinn grabbed her waist and flipped her beneath him. He slowly stood and started walking away from her.

"You can't make me play by the rules," Lily called.

"Turkey for Thanksgiving, ham for Christmas," Quinn said over his shoulder. "And I hate cranberries."

Lily sank back into the water. "I love cranberries," she murmured.

She scrambled to her feet. "And I hate sweet potatoes," she shouted. Lily cursed softly as she watched his retreat. Maybe he was right. Maybe they *should* know a bit more about each other before they jumped into a sexual relationship. But there weren't that many things that could change her mind about her desire for him.

So he hated cranberries. What other revelations would cause her to reconsider? Lily thought for a long moment before her breath caught in her throat.

Was this his way of warning her off him? If he really was a lawyer, as she'd suspected all along, was he trying to do the honorable thing and keep his distance? She'd planned to test him by asking him legal questions. But maybe he'd just revealed exactly the kind of man Quinn James truly was...

She waded out of the water and picked up her dress from the sand. As she tugged it over her head, she thought about her plans for the day. Maybe it would be best to stop daydreaming about Quinn and focus on her work.

It was time to start a new painting. And she knew exactly who she wanted her subject to be.

TRISTAN WASN'T REALLY sure what critique group was going to be all about. He expected to read a short passage from "his" novel and then the group would discuss it, giving him constructive criticism, before they moved on to another member of the group. He never, ever expected it to resemble the Spanish Inquisition.

From the moment the group sat down around the table in the dining hall, they'd turned on the metaphorical spotlight, shined it directly on him and begun with the questions. How long had he been writing? How many manuscripts had he completed before he started the current one? Had he ever submitted his work to a publisher? Had he studied writing in college? How many hours did he write each day?

Tristan tried as best he could to formulate believable answers, and when he couldn't, he offered something vague or deftly changed the subject and asked a question of his own.

He thought he was almost out of the woods, when they turned their attention to his work. After just a few minutes he was completely lost. A long discussion of "point of view" dissolved into an argument and then became physical when one of the writers tossed his pages across the table and told the group that they were all being pedantic.

It was at that point that Finch called an end to Quinn's critique and asked the group to move on to another member. Since no one else had anything to offer, the meeting ended and the participants scattered, a few of them still arguing their points.

Tristan gathered up the pages that the group had left while Finch cleaned up the coffee cups. "That was pretty brutal," he murmured.

Finch shrugged. "You have to be able to defend your work. If you can't, you have no business writing."

"It's a novel, not a cure to cancer."

"It's your work," Finch said. "Or is it?"

"What's that supposed to mean?" Tristan asked.

"Sit down, Quinn," Finch said, indicating a chair across the table from him.

Tristan did as he was told, and Finch took the opposite chair. "I've read a lot of first novels. Taught writing in a lot of colleges and universities. And over time, I've developed a sense for what we often call 'writer's voice.' It's another word for style. It's like a writer's fingerprint. Everyone is different. The rhythms, the choice of words, the personality that you find in the writing."

"What are you saying?" Tristan asked. "You don't like my style?"

"I don't believe you wrote this," Finch said. "In fact, I'd say this manuscript was written by a woman."

"You can tell that in just twenty-five pages?"

"I can," he said. "Am I right?"

Tristan drew a ragged breath. "I guess I shouldn't be surprised that someone would figure it out."

"Why would you come here pretending to be a writer? And where did you get the manuscript? Because it is really good."

"The manuscript belongs to a friend," he said. "And you're right. It was written by a woman. My coworker Melanie."

"If the full manuscript is as good as the first twenty-five pages, then she has a book to sell. I can steer her in the direction of a few good agents."

"I'm sure she'd appreciate that," Tristan murmured.

A long silence grew between them. "Are you going to tell me the rest?" Finch asked. "The real reason you're hanging around?"

"It started as one thing and now it's turned into something completely different," Tristan admitted.

"You need to tell her," Finch said. "I don't care what your reasons are but you have to be real with Lily. Even if it will ruin things for you."

"Maybe I should just leave the colony," Tristan said.

Finch slowly stood. "You don't strike me as the type of man who has ever taken the easy path. Why start now?"

Tristan watched the older man walk to the door, then out onto the porch.

His mind searched for a solution to his problems. How could he come clean about who he was and why he was here and still maintain his connection to Lily?

Perhaps if he could show her that he wasn't here to rob her great-aunts. He could find a way to provide the sisters with some help. Maybe they weren't completely against the deal they'd been offered. Maybe they just needed a negotiator who could get them exactly what they wanted.

Tristan buried his head in his hands, knowing that no matter what he did after telling Lily the truth, he'd still have to take the blame for the lie. He'd tricked Lily into inviting him here and he'd been lying about himself ever since then. No one could easily accept that.

The silence in the dining hall was suddenly interrupted by the frantic clanging of the bell outside.

Tristan strode to the door and before he could open it, Lily came running inside.

"What's wrong?" he asked.

Her color was high and her hair wild, but it was the grim expression on her face that concerned him.

"Come outside," she said.

He followed her through the door and found the populace of the colony gathering. A few seconds later, the three sisters pulled up in a vintage Cadillac convertible, Violet behind the wheel.

"How much time do we have?" Lily asked.

"Ten minutes, maybe fifteen," Daisy said.

"All right, everyone. Let's get the cars and create the blockade, right where we stopped them the last time. Finch and Bernie, get the guns. Ladies, bring the signs. But remember, we're just standing up for our rights here. And we'll do it peacefully."

Tristan grabbed Lily's arm. "What's going on?"

"We need your car. Do you have your keys with you?"

"First tell me what's going on," he insisted.

"The sheriff is on his way. I don't know what he wants, but the last time he came, he tried to arrest the aunts for trespassing on their own property."

Tristan turned to find Finch and Bernie emerging from the dining halls with their arms full of hunting rifles and shotguns. They quickly passed them around to both the men and the women. A few moments later, more cars arrived and everyone hopped in and headed toward the colony entrance.

Tristan ran to get his car. When he got back, he was

at the end of a very strange line of vehicles. Finch was behind the wheel of a classic Mustang. Bernie drove a Prius. There was also a Volkswagen bus, an old MG sports car, a rusted Volvo station wagon and a battered 1950s pickup truck hauling a rusted generator.

The caravan stopped near the end of the drive, very close to where Tristan had met Lily two days ago. The drivers arranged the cars so that no others could pass, parking at odd angles over the entire width of the road. Tristan parked the Mercedes and then hopped out and hurried to where Lily stood.

"Here, take this," she said, shoving an old pistol into his hand.

"Guns? What are you thinking? Someone could get killed."

"No one is going to get killed," she said.

"How can you know that? The sheriff could—"

"We don't have any bullets," she said. "Besides, the sheriff was the one who suggested the guns. He said we needed some props that made us look more threatening."

Though Tristan knew exactly what this was about, as far as Lily was aware, he knew nothing. "What are we protesting?" he asked.

"No one's told you?" Lily asked.

"I've only been here a few days. I guess I'm not part of the club yet."

"My family is trying to take this land away from my aunts. The lake, the property around it and their three houses were a gift from their father. But according to the rest of the family, the gift was never put on paper and everything belongs in the family trust."

"Can't you take it to court?"

"We've been told that our case is weak. So we've been trying to avoid court."

"And this is your lawyer's strategy? What kind of lawyer do you have?"

Lily sighed. "Not a very good one. No one wants to take our case. They say it's unwinnable. We figure if we just hold out, maybe my family will get tired of the bother and give up."

"What do they want to do?"

"They want to sell the land and invest in the development of a huge resort and water park complex. They'll surround the lake with condo cottages and this place will never be the same again. And I love it just like this. Simple. The way it was when I was a little girl. The way it was when I discovered my passion for art."

Tristan took in the tense expression that clouded her pretty features. How had he ever thought he was on the right side of this case? When he'd first been briefed about the details, it had seemed like a slam dunk. Without a signed deed or any evidence that the property had ever been a gift, they had no case. But was evidence the only thing that mattered? Was his own ambition any less greedy than the Harrisons'?

"And the aunts. They're all determined to stay?"

"They love this place. You've seen them. Do you really think they'll fit in anywhere else? Here, they can be themselves. Out there, people would call them crazy."

"Here he comes!"

"Remember," Lily called. "Don't smile for the cameras! Look tough. Determined. A little mean."

Everyone scrambled to form a line in front of the cars, two squad cars and a red Ford sedan. The sheriff got out of the car and the crowd immediately began to shout.

"Hell, no, we won't go. Hell, no, we won't go."

The sheriff held up his hands for silence and when he didn't get it, one of the deputies handed him a bullhorn. "I'm not here to stir things up. I'm just here to serve Violet, Rose and Daisy Pigglestone with eviction papers. Ladies, if you'd come up here, I'll just hand you these documents, we'll get a quick two or three photos and I'll be on my way."

The crowd continued to chant and wave their signs as the three sisters posed for pictures. It was all a very strange scene, staged for the single photographer. Tristan had to wonder what else the group was doing to prepare for the fight ahead.

Once he had given them the papers, the sheriff drove off. Lily retrieved the papers from her aunts and slipped behind the wheel of his car. She held out her hand for the keys, wiggling her fingers until he surrendered them.

He jumped into the passenger seat just as she threw the car into gear. Taking the lead in the line of cars, she headed back into camp. Tristan reached out and grabbed the papers she'd stuck next to the console. As the sheriff had said, the papers were indeed eviction notices for the three Pigglestone sisters.

"How much time did they give us to pack up this time?" she asked, her hair snapping in the wind.

"This time?"

"We've gotten two or three eviction notices before. The dates are different every time. I have all the papers in a box. I've saved everything they send us."

"Lily, this is really serious. What are you doing to make a case for yourself?"

"What do you mean?"

"Ignoring the problem won't make it go away. You need to prepare yourself for a fight. You have to gather evidence that will prove your claim on the property in court. This is all going to take a lot of work."

She pulled the car up in front of the dining hall and shut off the ignition. "I know," she murmured. "I've tried to convince my aunts that we have to fight my family in court, but when I talk to them, they get upset."

"They need to know the truth," he said. Tristan drew a deep breath. "Would you like me to help you? I'm a lawyer. I could advise you."

Lily glanced over at him and he could see she was startled by his offer. "We have a lawyer. Two, in fact," she said.

"And it doesn't seem as if either of them are doing you much good. You should hire someone closer to the situation."

A moment later, she nodded. "All right. I suppose we could try that and see how it goes. Sometimes it does seem a bit overwhelming, and the pressure can be too much."

"Well, I might be able to do something about that," Tristan said.

He pressed a kiss to her forehead, then got out of the car. Though everything about this screamed conflict of interest, Tristan was increasingly beginning to doubt he was on the right side of this case.

He hadn't gotten into law to line a rich man's pockets. He'd wanted to fight for people who couldn't fight for themselves. People like him and his brothers. Like Lily and her great-aunts.

The law would consider them squatters. But squatters had rights, and more often than not, those rights led to possession of the property. There was no way the family foundation would let a multimillion-dollar property go without a fight. But he might be able to help even the odds.

Once he knew where the ladies stood, he could decide if the offer he'd brought was their best option or if they should stand and fight for the place they loved so much.

"I want you to show me everything," he said.

4

THEY SAT IN the small office at the far end of the dining hall, surrounded by knotty pine paneling and piles of papers that Quinn had made all over the floor. Lily hadn't realized how many times the sisters had received legal notices over the past few years about the property, nor had she recognized the escalating urgency contained within each piece of correspondence.

She handed Quinn the last piece of their problem, the eviction notices that the sheriff had delivered that morning. He glanced up. "That's it?"

Lily nodded.

"That's every piece of paper you've received? There's nothing with the aunts, nothing you sent the lawyer and forgot to copy?"

"This is it. I'm certain."

Quinn sat back on his heels and sighed, taking in the three hours of work he'd just completed. "Lily, there are court orders here that have been left unanswered. At any moment, a judge could order you or the aunts arrested for contempt. There have been hearings scheduled that you've ignored."

"My family would never have us arrested. The scandal and shame would be too much."

"The judge might," he said. "It's very clear from all of this that you four are going to have to face this head-on by making your case in court. Hopefully that will be enough to keep the land."

"My great-aunts are over seventy years old," Lily said. "Fighting in court could kill them." She crawled across the floor, sat down next to him and leaned in to see what he was reading.

She still wasn't sure she could completely trust him, but over the course of the afternoon, she'd come to respect his honesty and his patience. He didn't pull any punches. Quinn had told her exactly how difficult the case was going to be. He'd talked about squatter's rights and how he'd approach the case. Everything he said made perfect sense and pointed to his good character.

"Your aunts are a lot stronger than you think they are," he said.

"I can't show all of this to them. They'll freak out."

Quinn glanced from pile to pile, then picked each one up and stacked them neatly in front of him. Spread apart, they hadn't seemed quite so intimidating as the mound in front of him. From the expression on Quinn's face, Lily could tell they were in serious trouble.

She wanted to cast aside all of her worries, if only for a little while. She could trust Quinn with that at least. "Take me to bed," she murmured, wrapping her arms around his neck. "Make love to me, Quinn."

He groaned softly. "Lily, there's so much more to do here. We can't stop now."

"We'll come back to it," she said. "Tomorrow, we'll look at it with fresh eyes. Tonight, we'll pretend it doesn't exist."

Quinn gently grabbed her by the arms and set her beside him. "And that's exactly why you're in the trouble you are. You can't make your problems disappear just by closing your eyes."

"You don't have to tell me that. You sound just like my father, and I don't need another father." She scrambled to her feet. "Since I'm so irresponsible maybe you should stop spending so much time with me."

Quinn cursed softly. "I know you're not irresponsible. You've proved that on more than one occasion. But having sex with me is also not going to solve your problems. It may be distracting and a lot of fun for the moment, but this will all be here when it's over."

"There are moments when I wonder if you're avoiding me."

"We're together all the time."

"I'm talking about sex. I know you're attracted to me. Any other man would jump at the chance. No strings, no expectations. Just sex. What is it? Don't you like women?"

Quinn got to his feet. "This conversation borders on the ridiculous. And all of the stress has made you a little crazy."

Lily's temper began to rise and for the first time in

her life she wanted to spit out something pointed and hurtful. She'd always been so careful before she spoke to make sure everything she said was true and kind. But now she actually wanted to hurt another human being. To sting him the way that he had stung her. "Well, you certainly don't want to sleep with a crazy person. So I guess I'll head back to my cabin and get a good night's sleep."

She strode out of the room, ignoring the three people who were playing cards at a nearby table in the dining hall. They'd obviously heard the entire conversation and the gossip would be all around camp before sunrise. But she was beyond caring. It was clear that Quinn had never truly wanted her. He'd toyed with her, like a cat might play with a mouse, but he'd never intended to take it any further.

"Lily!" he shouted. "Come on. I know you're stressed and you didn't mean what you said."

"I meant every word," she shouted. "Just leave me alone!" She walked out the door, letting it slam behind her, then headed toward her studio. She'd been wasting far too much time with this romance, Lily told herself. It had upset the rhythms of her life and thrown her mind into a constant state of chaos.

Usually, she had no trouble handling no-strings affairs, keeping everything in perspective. In fact, Lily had always prided herself on her ability to separate her sex life from her personal life. Though she couldn't seem to separate it from her professional life.

Good sex—deep and passionate sex—had led to

some of the most creative moments of her life. She'd thought she could have that again with Quinn.

"Lily!"

"Go away," she warned.

"No. I have something to say to you."

"I don't want to hear it. You've insulted me enough for one night."

He finally caught up with her, then grabbed her hand and spun her around to face him. "I need you to hear this. Then you can go to bed."

"Make it quick," she muttered, refusing to meet his gaze.

Quinn reached down and hooked his thumb beneath her chin. "Look at me," he whispered. "I do want you. I haven't been able to stop thinking about how good we'd be together." He let his hand drift down her shoulder to her breast. Slowly, he teased at her nipple beneath the faded fabric of her dress, until it grew to a hard peak.

Her pulse raced and for a moment, she felt positively giddy. But then Lily remembered what he'd said to her. "I'm not irresponsible," she muttered. "I may choose to look at life in an overly positive manner, but that doesn't make me a flake."

"I'm well aware that you're not a flake." He dropped a kiss on her lips, his tongue just touching her fleetingly before he drew back. His hands drifted lower until he could catch the upper part of her skirt. When her legs were revealed, he slipped his fingers between them, slowly stroking her outer folds. "Don't underestimate the power you have over me, Lily."

"What difference does it make?" she asked.

"If we take that step, if we surrender it's going to be like—like a wildfire. Out of control. Consuming. That's never happened to me before. It scares me a little, I'll admit."

"You're afraid of me?"

He drew a sharp breath, then reluctantly nodded. "I know it doesn't make much sense. But it can't be casual between us, Lily. It has to be full-on, no-holds-barred passion or nothing at all. Because once we make love, neither one of us is going to forget it." He drove his hand deeper into the soft flesh, then slowly drew it away. "Are you ready for that, Lily? I'm not."

A shudder raced through her and she twisted out of his hold. Stumbling back, she gasped for a breath that would clear her head and return her ability to think again.

"The world would change, Lily."

Trembling, Lily hurried up the path, praying that this time he wouldn't follow her. From the moment they'd met, she'd sensed a physical attraction that neither of them wanted to deny. But suddenly, he'd changed his mind and found her too dangerous.

She wasn't asking for anything more than simple pleasure. But that was too much for him. Lily raced up the porch steps of her cabin and slipped inside. Leaning back against the rough plank door, she tried to regain her breath and her composure.

A soft rap sounded on the other side of the door. "Lily? Let me in."

"Just go away," she said. "I'll talk to you tomorrow."

"I'm sorry," Quinn said. "I didn't mean to hurt you.

"You didn't hurt me," she lied. "I'm fine. I'll talk to you tomorrow." Lily held her breath, waiting, wondering if he'd give up or insist on coming inside. After a long wait, she slowly opened the door and found the porch empty.

Lily held back a sob but she couldn't keep the tears from flooding her eyes. Why was this so emotional for her? She hadn't trusted him from the start. He was a lawyer and in her experience, lawyers were notoriously untrustworthy.

She'd been lonely and vulnerable and she'd fallen for him because he'd been convenient...and charming... and sexy.

Frustrated, Lily quickly brushed the tears from her cheeks. She'd been perfectly fine without him before he'd arrived and she'd be fine again when he left.

"OH, MY," DAISY said as she took in the piles in front of her. "This does appear to be a daunting task. But I hate to ask our guests to help. This is our problem, not theirs."

Tristan shook his head. "Where are they going to go each summer if this place closes down? They have as much to lose as you ladies do. And I'm sure they'd be happy to lend a hand, especially if it means saving the colony."

The four long tables in the dining hall were stacked with old crates, boxes and several pieces of luggage. Mixed in were musty ledger books and bundles of manila folders tied with twine. Tristan and the aunts had scoured every corner of the camp looking for every last piece of paperwork that had been saved over the years. "If we're lucky, the proof for your claim is buried in these boxes and bundles."

Violet chuckled. "We aren't much for minding our business interests," she said. "There's always been plenty of money."

Tristan had come across their bank statement and had been stunned by the fact that they kept over a million dollars in ready cash yet weren't aware of the balance. He couldn't help but remember the awful struggles of his childhood, searching for spare change to buy a gallon of milk or a package of hot dogs—anything to stave off the hunger.

To have so much money that you never had to count it would have been an amazing luxury, something that would have changed his life and altered his destiny. His parents would have been happy, they would have stayed married. They all would have lived in a fine home on a quiet street in a safe neighborhood. And rather than fighting to survive nearly every single day, he and his brothers could have focused on school and sports. They could have had a childhood.

But that didn't mean the sisters weren't any less deserving of his help.

"Where is Lily?" Rose asked. "She's usually up and about at this hour."

"Why don't we ring the bell," Tristan said. "She'll probably come then."

Daisy hurried to the porch off the dining hall and began to sound the camp bell. The bright, clear sound pierced the late morning air and before long, people began to wander inside, curious about the cause of the summons.

Tristan kept his gaze fixed on the door, waiting for Lily, wondering if she'd acknowledge him or simply avoid his gaze. When she finally did appear, he felt the breath leave his body. She looked extraordinarily beautiful this morning, dressed in a pale blue skirt and a camisole that revealed her deeply tanned belly.

She glanced his way and he saw a smile brighten her expression for a fleeting second. Their gazes locked as she slowly approached, gracefully weaving between the others. But at the last moment, she turned to her aunts and took her place between them, out of the reach of both his touch and his sight.

When everyone was settled, Tristan stepped forward. "Good morning. As most of you know, the Pigglestone sisters have been caught up in a legal battle over ownership of this beautiful property, the lake, the land around it and their artists' colony. With every week that passes, the fight becomes more aggressive and it now looks like the sisters are going to have to step up and fight their battle in court."

"What can we do to help?" Finch asked.

"That's why I've brought you here. We have to find some proof that this land was always meant to be deeded to the sisters. If we can't find absolute proof, we have to show intent. So, I have a list of tasks we need to do in order to build the case and we'd appreciate your help to complete this on time. Those of you who would like to help should stay. Those who don't may leave."

Tristan paused. No one in the room moved an inch.

He took a deep breath. "All right, I need two people to visit the register of deeds at the county courthouse and copy the entire file on this property."

Finch raised his hand. "I can do that," he said. "Who wants to come with me?" Billy Chadwick-Farnsworth volunteered and the two of them walked out together.

"I also need two people to go to the library and go through the early newspaper indexes. Pull anything that mentions the Pigglestone sisters or their father." Two more people volunteered. After he assigned a few more tasks he motioned for Bernie to come forward.

"Bernie, I know you've got some skills researching on the internet." He handed the writer a piece of paper. "Her name was Luella Helmsworth. She was Edward Pigglestone's secretary until his death. If she's still alive, she'd be about eighty. We need to find her."

Bernie nodded and hurried out the door. The rest of the residents set to work on the piles of correspondence on the tables. He walked over to the sisters and smiled. "It's a good start," he said. "But you three should sit down and write out all your recollections of what your father told you about this land. As close as you can, I want you to reconstruct his words and his intentions. Write it all down."

"We don't know how to possibly thank you," Violet said. She stepped up and gave him a hug, then patted him on the back as she kissed his cheek. Daisy and Rose followed suit before turning and waiting for Lily to do the same.

"Go make a pot of tea and get to work," Lily said. "I'll be along in a few minutes to help you."

When they'd left, Lily took his hand and drew him along to the old office, then pulled him inside and closed the door. Lily drew a ragged breath, then looked up at him. "I'm sorry about last night."

"That wasn't you," he quickly said. "That was me. I'm the one who is sorry. I said a lot of things I didn't mean."

"You might not have meant them, but you told the truth. It was never going to be simple between us and I've wondered whether we were foolish to believe—"

"Maybe optimistic would be a better word."

"Maybe," Lily said. "But that doesn't mean I don't—"

"Care," he finished. "I do, too. My feelings haven't changed."

"I'm not afraid to be afraid," Lily said. "It feels right to be with you. I'm just scared that it's all going to end before I want it to."

It was much more complex for Tristan. He was still playing a part, pretending to be someone he wasn't. And though he'd redeemed his character a bit by his recent good deeds, there would still come a day when he'd have to tell the truth. And the truth was bound to hurt Lily.

He'd spent all of last night turning the situation over in his mind, trying to find a way to escape his dilemma without destroying his relationship with Lily. He'd come to one conclusion. He wasn't going to admit the truth until he was absolutely sure that it wouldn't make a difference to her.

"Can we just rewind? Let's just forget everything we said."

"I don't care about the past," Lily said, "and I don't care about the future. We don't have to involve or emotions. I just want to be with you today, in the present. Is that what you want? Because if it is, then I think you should kiss me."

Tristan smiled at the stubborn look on her face. "Now?"

"Now," she said.

"Not…in five minutes?"

"No, now."

"Oops, I guess I missed that chance. It just flew right by."

Lily took his face between her hands and pressed a kiss to his lips. He wrapped his arm around her waist and pulled her closer, then deepened the kiss, his tongue gently teasing until she surrendered completely.

This felt right, Tristan thought, as her fingertips danced across his chest. His entire world fell into place when he was with Lily. She was like a weather vane that pointed him in the right direction each day. This way to happiness.

"Is this my job?" Lily asked. "To keep the captain happy?"

"As much as I'd love to assign you such an important task, I have something else for you to do. I need you to keep the aunts in good spirits. Talk to them about the past. Find anything that might be used to get the media interested in this place. Famous former guests, prize-winning books that were written here, titillating scandals, anything that might cause people to side with us."

"Us?"

"The society dedicated to the preservation of the Fence Lake Artists' Colony." He chuckled softly. "There's another task. Come up with an appropriate name. Once we do that, we'll set up a fundraising source on the internet and start to collect funds from old friends and supporters."

Lily drew a deep breath. "Kissing you would be so much more enjoyable."

Tristan gave her a hug. "There will be time for that, I promise. Now, I have some very important work to do. I'll see you later."

He moved to the door and pulled it open. "Do you really think we can win this?" Lily asked, staring up at him, a desperate glint in her eyes.

"I think we can make an argument. How good that argument is will depend on us."

"Thank you, Quinn, for coming to our rescue. You're a good man."

"Go ahead, I'll meet up with you later."

Lily pushed up on her toes and gave him a kiss on the cheek. "Later."

Tristan watched her leave, then walked out to the table and grabbed his laptop. He found a place to sit, then opened a new document.

This letter is to notify the firm of Foster and Dunlap that I, Tristan Quinn, resign my position as an associate attorney, effective immediately. Due to unforeseen circumstances, I will no longer be able to effectively represent the interests of the firm.

The moment the words were written, Tristan felt an instant calm wash over him. From a business standpoint, he could proceed with a clear mind. But until he told Lily the whole truth, his personal life would still be a tangle of unspoken desires and hidden motives, so twisted that he wasn't sure how he could sort it out.

LILY SAT ON an upholstered chair, an old journal open on her lap. She recognized Aunt Violet's handwriting scrawled across the pages. From the moment the three sisters had opened their artists' colony, Violet had kept meticulous records of all the artists who had visited.

She slowly scanned the lists, each name matched up with dates and an assigned cabin. Her gaze found one name that stood out. "This O. Richards," she said. "Is that *the* O. Richards? The famous actor?"

Violet sat up and considered the question for a long moment. "I suppose it was."

"Oscar Richards stayed here at the colony?"

"Yes," Violet said.

"He's important. Were there others?"

"It's hard for me to remember, darling. Everyone seemed important at the time. There was that playwright… Daisy, you remember. He loved to fish. Insisted on eating everything he caught."

"That *was* a time," Violet said with a smile. "For ten or fifteen years, our little colony was the place to be. They'd come for a week or two and live like ordinary folk. Oh, do you remember that one woman who we were all convinced was that Hollywood starlet but she would never give us her real name?"

Daisy giggled. "Oh, I do!"

"We were never sure if we were right about who she really was. A family emergency called her home early."

"Well, we did have that strange man who claimed to be Andy Warhol. Just insisted. We all knew he wasn't but we let him stay. He was quite entertaining."

"This would make a wonderful book," Lily murmured. "Or a documentary." She closed the journal on her lap. "I could call Robert."

"Robert Burke?" Daisy clapped her hands. "Oh, I loved him. He was so handsome and so talented. You were lovers, weren't you, Lily?"

"Yes," she said. "We were." She quickly stood, then gave her aunts each a kiss on the cheek. "Keep working and write some of these things down. I'm going to check in with Quinn."

Lily ran down to the dining hall, a clever idea beginning to form in her head. Though it required calling on an ex-lover, their circumstances were dire. She was willing to sacrifice her personal comfort.

She opened the dining room door and stuck her head inside. "Is Quinn in here?"

"He left about an hour ago," Finch called.

"Thanks," Lily said. She checked the rec hall and his cabin but he was nowhere to be found. His car was still parked where she'd left it. She decided to check her studio. As she walked along the path, she glanced out at the sun-splashed surface of the lake. He was there, bobbing in the water about twenty yards offshore.

Lily stood next to a tree, watching him through a bower of green. For a long time, he floated quietly on his back, his face turned up to the sky, his limbs relaxed. And then, suddenly, he'd submerge and swim to some other spot, popping up when he ran out of breath.

When he started toward the shore, Lily walked out of the woods and onto the beach, her eyes shaded by her hand. He smiled when he saw her and she waved, trying to ignore the fact that he was naked.

"Have you been spying on me?" he teased.

"Of course. I've always admired the view from this spot."

He stepped up to her, then shook his wet head, the droplets splattering onto her dry skin. Then, with a chuckle, he bent close and kissed her. "Were you going to swim? I'd be happy to watch."

He grabbed a towel from beneath the pile of clothes he'd left and spread it out on the narrow strip of sand. Then he sat down, brushing the sand off his hands. He patted the spot beside him. "Sit," he said. "Relax."

"It's such a beautiful day," Lily said. "It's hard to believe there'll be snow falling soon."

"It must be nice here in the winter, too," he said.

Lily nodded. "Like a fairy tale. I got caught up here last fall in a three-day blizzard. I stayed with Violet. Daisy and Rose had already left to visit friends in San Diego. We had such an amazing time."

"Have you thought about what you'll do if they can't keep this place?"

Lily shook her head. "I can't let myself think about it. It would kill me if I let it happen."

"It's not your fault. You can't control your family. And you can't change the past."

She slipped her arm around his and leaned her head on his shoulder. "Have I thanked you for everything you're doing for us? If I haven't, thank you." Lily kissed his cheek. "I was thinking we could go into town tonight and have dinner. My treat. I'll take you to my favorite spot. It's this old roadhouse that serves the best steaks. Would you like that?"

"Is this a date?"

"This would qualify as a date, yes. As long as we have a bottle of wine with dinner."

"And after dinner I'm going to seduce you," Quinn said.

"I'm beginning to wonder if you're one of those guys who likes talking about sex more than he likes having sex," Lily teased.

"Ow!" Quinn cried, falling back onto the towel. He threw his arm over his eyes. "Do such men exist?"

Lily leaned over him, resting her arm on his chest. "I've never met one until now."

He sat up, bracing his hands behind him. "It's just that I'm out of my element with you. I'm used to seduction being dangerous. But you seem to take a more…"

"Organic?" she said.

"I was going to say an *adventurous* approach to relationships."

"It's just sex," she said.

"It's never just sex," Quinn said in a low voice.

"You're a very complicated man, Quinn."

"You have no idea," he said.

They lay in the sun until it began to dip behind the trees behind them and the chill of the evening set in.

Lily told him about the discoveries she'd made in Violet's journal, about the famous people who'd visited the colony in years past.

"That's good, but we'll also need money to create publicity," he said. "The aunts have to decide how much they're willing to sacrifice in order to save this place."

Lily shook her head. "No. I don't want them to worry about that. I have money. We can use that."

"Lily, your aunts are quite well off. And I think, between the three of them, they can afford to hire a publicist who can create some media presence for them. They're made for television. And once people learn their story, it's going to be hard for the family to throw them off the property, even if it doesn't belong to them."

"I don't think the trustees would settle for that."

"There is another option," he said. "You could pool your money and buy the property from the foundation. It would probably take most of what you have, but the property would be yours."

"It is ours now," Lily said stubbornly. "I'm not going to buy something that my aunts already own."

Lily had always tried to think positive, to be optimistic about her future. But after talking to Quinn about their legal problems, she realized that he was preparing her for the worst. He was a professional, an attorney with some knowledge of real estate law, and he was gently steering her toward the truth. Her life in this beautiful place, with her three precious aunts, might be coming to an end.

If it was just her, Lily knew she'd be able to move

on. But Violet, Rose and Daisy had built their lives around the colony. It was the only place where they could be completely free to be themselves.

But there would come a day when they'd be gone, when her time with them would be just faded memories. Would she be all alone? Or would there be someone in her life—a husband or children—she could love?

She had always admired the aunts and their fierce independence. They'd lived their lives on their own terms, never allowing society to make their choices for them. From her youngest years, Lily had always assumed she'd end up just like them—alone, but happy. But since Quinn had arrived, those visions of her future had been shifting and changing.

Maybe she wasn't meant to spend her life alone. Maybe this man, or the next, was the one who'd capture her heart and build a life with her. It had always been a simple matter to discard her lovers, especially when she'd believed that her future would be free of husbands and hangers-on. But the more she thought about her future, the more she wondered if Quinn was supposed to be part of it.

Life seemed to speeding up. For now, she was still hopeful, but Lily felt as if everything was about to start careening out of control, heading for a huge crash that would claim too many victims.

5

"WATCH THOSE EGGS," Finch said. "Low and slow. You don't want them to get brown on the bottom."

Tristan checked the frying pan, then moved over to the griddle where he'd been frying bacon. "Why don't you give me a hand here? I'm making breakfast for the both of us."

"I'd rather watch you," Finch said. "What else can you make? We could work out a nice deal here. I'll buy all the food if you do all the cooking."

"You're looking for a cook," Tristan said.

"I don't need a cook. My wife's a genius in the kitchen. She lives in Panama City, Florida, with our children and grandchildren. Put that toast down or it won't be done with the rest of the food."

"How does that work?" Tristan asked. "Your wife is all right with you spending the whole summer up here?"

"Sure. When we were younger, we spent all our time together, but as we got older, we developed our own interests and routines. Marriage is about compromise and flexibility. You have to write your own rules as you go along. If you try to follow someone else's design, you're setting yourself up for failure."

Tristan had never thought much about marriage. He hadn't grown up in a made-for-television family with an encouraging father and a sympathetic mother. He wouldn't know where to start, he mused as he carefully flipped the eggs. "My brother has himself a fiancée. I guess they'll be getting married. They seem to be a good match."

"Quinn! Quinn, are you in here?"

Lily's voice echoed through the dining hall. "I'm in the kitchen making breakfast," Tristan called.

She appeared in the doorway. Her hair was tousled and there was a black smudge on her cheek. As always, she wore a loose cotton shift and no shoes. "You have to come with me," she said, breathless, her color high in her cheeks.

"What?"

"Just come. Right now. It's really important."

"I'm making breakfast. Can it wait a few minutes?"

"No, it might be gone already." She turned and walked to the door, her shoulders slumped.

Tristan glanced between the breakfast and a sadly dejected Lily. His stomach growled in protest and he cursed softly. "You better take over," he said to Finch. "I'll go see what she wants."

By the time he got outside, she was already running up the path toward her studio. He followed her at a steady pace, wondering what had gotten her into such a state so early in the day.

He and Lily had fallen into a pattern of sorts over the past week, spending their days in solitude before coming together after the sun went down. He'd meet her at her studio, or on the beach, and the night would be theirs. And though they'd developed an easy and comfortable relationship, their sex life had been moving at a glacial speed.

In truth, Tristan had his reasons for holding back. There were still so many lies between them, and his conscience wouldn't allow him to take advantage of her in any way. He fought the urge to surrender to her touch nearly every night, knowing that until she could call him by his real name, until she could look into his eyes and see the man he really was, they could only play at sex like a couple of teenagers.

Surprisingly, Lily didn't seem to be too concerned over the lack of sexual intimacy. Perhaps it was because everything between them seemed so much more powerful because they were going slow.

"Really?" He placed a foot on the step and waited for her to appear above him. When she did, she wasn't smiling.

"Get up here!" she cried.

"What's so urgent?" Tristan asked. "I didn't get to eat my breakfast."

"Your breakfast can wait."

Tristan slowly climbed the stairs and when he came level with the floor, he saw that her studio was in disarray. Pads of paper were scattered across the floor with crumpled pieces in between them. From the floor, he picked up a piece of charcoal, whittled to a point, and returned it to a small tin can on her desk.

They'd had dinner out the previous night and as Lily had promised, it had been perfectly romantic. Afterward, they'd gone to Lily's studio. One bottle of wine had turned to two, and they'd talked and laughed and learned the tiniest details of each other's lives, though Quinn was reluctant to give her many details about his childhood.

They fell asleep on the daybed in the corner, surrounded by the drape of mosquito netting and lit only by the soft glow from a kerosene lamp. When he left early this morning, she'd still been asleep and the studio had been in a tidy state.

"Stand right there," she said. "Right there in that spill of light." Lily waited until he had done as instructed, her arms crossed over her chest. "Now turn to the left. No, no, no. To the right."

"Lily, what is this about?"

"Last night, I woke up and spent an hour just watching you sleep. And I realized what I had to do. What I was meant to do. It was right there in front of me. I got up and made some drawings." With trembling fingers she smoothed her hair from her face. "I'm running out of time with this place and my art. I have to do this now or I may never have the chance—or the courage—again."

"That's crazy. Of course you will."

Lily shook her head. "No. I can feel it draining out of me. Take your clothes off."

The moment had finally come, but there were so many lies still standing between them, so many deceptions. He wanted a clean slate, nothing that might lead to regrets. He wanted to soar with the exhilaration that her body provided and not wallow in guilt. He might have only one chance and he didn't want to make a mess of it.

He slowly removed his clothes, tossing aside his T-shirt and stepping out of his flip-flops and cargo shorts. Like Lily, Tristan was becoming a minimalist when it came to clothes. He'd stopped wearing underwear a few days ago and chose his wardrobe by the fabrics that would feel best against his naked skin. He waited for a moment, then smiled. "Now you," he murmured.

"The artist usually stays dressed," Lily said. "It's the model who gets naked."

A strange flood of relief washed over him. This wasn't about seduction, this was about art. "You want to draw me?"

"I want to paint you," she corrected. "But first I have to make some drawings."

The prospect of spending the morning in her presence, completely naked, and possibly aroused, felt undeniably erotic. He decided to give himself over to her artistic process. "What do you want me to do?"

"Stand against that wall," she said, "and brace your arms above your head. Then shift one foot back until the muscles in your calves and thighs are tight."

He did as she ordered, then glanced over his shoulder to make sure she was pleased. Tristan caught her staring at him, her eyes wide and her lips parted. He flexed his muscles across his shoulders and shifted the other foot back. "Maybe this is better."

"Yes, that's fine. Just like that."

He could feel her eyes on his body, taking in every detail before committing it to paper. It was like being caressed by an invisible touch, as tantalizing as her fingers or lips or tongue would have been. He let his mind wander as she continued to draw, fantasizing about where this session could lead.

Still, it was enough to warm his blood and make him hard. And when she finally ordered him to turn around, the task was met by an audible gasp the moment her gaze took in his erection.

"Sorry," he said. "Do you want me with or without?"

She blinked, her gaze still fixed on his crotch as if it was the first time she'd ever seen him aroused. Tristan imagined that she was having as much trouble as he was focusing on the task at hand, even though she was trying to maintain an objective distance.

He reached down and slowly stroked himself, watching her reaction as he did. "So?"

"I think I can work with it," she murmured. "Why don't you go over to the daybed and lie down. I've got some other ideas."

As he walked across the room, Tristan felt strangely vulnerable. He ought to be able to control his desires and yet, in this highly charged atmosphere, all he could think about was sex. He imagined her body lying next to him on the bed, naked and willing, ready. And as she asked him to lie back and wrap his fingers around his shaft, he imagined her lips hovering just above the tip, her tongue ready to touch him and send him into spasms of sheer pleasure.

Tristan closed his eyes and listened to the strange scratch of her charcoal against the paper. He hadn't realized until now the erotic power of his imagination. It was possible to have an entire sexual adventure with Lily simply by closing his eyes.

Oh, hell, he thought to himself. If fantasy had the power to shatter his expectations, what would the real thing do to them? He slowly began to stroke himself. "Is this all right?" he asked.

When she didn't answer, Tristan opened his eyes. She was sitting absolutely still, watching him, her eyes wide, her lips slightly parted. She seemed to be enjoying the view, so Tristan decided to continue. Would she leave her sketchpad and charcoal and join him on the daybed? Or would she prefer to watch until he found release on his own?

For a long time, she just observed, occasionally drawing something on her sketchpad. He closed his eyes again, allowing himself to indulge in his own pleasure for a few minutes before returning his attention to her.

The next time he looked, her chair was empty. She stood at the end of the daybed, her gaze still fixed on him, drifting from his eyes to his hands. "Would you like to join me?" he asked.

Lily smiled. She reached for the buttons on her dress and slowly undid them. Brushing the faded cotton fabric from her shoulders, she let the garment drop to the floor around her feet.

A frisson of desire shot through him at the sight of her naked body. He stilled his stroke for a moment, not willing to lose control yet. He was suddenly ready, his nerves crackling with anticipation. Tristan imagined what her hands would feel like on his skin, caressing him closer and closer to completion.

But when Lily smoothed her palm down her belly and slipped her fingers into the folds between her legs, he realized that she'd misunderstood his offer. He wouldn't correct her, though. What she was doing was more tantalizing than anything in his imagination.

Tristan slowly began again, this time watching her move toward her own orgasm. She closed her eyes and ran her hands over her breasts. And when it was too much to stand, she stretched out at the opposite end of the daybed.

Tristan grabbed her ankle and pulled her closer, until he could brush aside her fingers and let his tongue take over.

Her body reacted, growing still, then her muscles arched and twisted as she tried to push herself closer to him. She cried out once and then dissolved into a series of sharp spasms.

He groaned as he fell back into the pillows on the bed, slowly stroking her leg. "Sorry," he said. "I guess I got a little distracted."

"It was a nice distraction," she said.

"I got you to take your dress off," he teased.

"Oh, is that what this was all about?"

"Of course. If I have to be naked, so do you. New rule, no exceptions."

LILY STARED AT the painting, her gaze shifting from the bright slashes of color to the nearly black shadows. She'd finished it yesterday, a bold nude of Quinn from behind—his arms raised over his head, his finely hewn shoulders and back, narrow hips and muscled legs.

"It's...powerful," Violet said.

"Emotional," Rose added.

"And strangely...erotic," Daisy finished breathlessly.

"It's the best work I've ever done. I felt it, like I was pouring out my soul onto the canvas. I wasn't even thinking, I was just painting, and this appeared before my eyes."

"It is...him?" Rose asked.

"Quinn? Yes. Although you really can't tell."

"Perhaps if you'd do a frontal view," Daisy said, "he might be more recognizable, hmm?"

"Yes," Violet said. "Absolutely. A frontal view would be preferable...for recognition purposes."

"Oh, I agree. Unless, of course, the frontal view might be a...a disappointment. Would it be?" Rose asked. "A disappointment?"

"Definitely not," Lily said with a grin. "I think I finally understand the power of this place," Lily said. "I've found my voice. My muse." She turned to the aunts. "We can't let them take this place from us. We have to do everything we can to save it."

Lily felt a powerful desperation surging up inside

her, a fear so deep that she was almost afraid to breathe. For years, she'd searched for the artist inside her. She'd tried so many different things, hoping that something would ignite her passion. Only in this place with this man had she found it.

"I'm working on another painting, and it might be even better than this one. It focuses more on the torso."

"We should show them to the rest of the camp," Violet said.

Lily shook her head. "Not yet. They're still too personal. I knew I could trust you three, but I don't want any criticism until I've had a chance to create a few more canvases. Maybe this is just a—a fluke?"

Violet slipped her arm around Lily's shoulders and gave her a hug. "This is what we've been waiting for. We knew you'd find it, Lily. Just like each of us discovered the artist inside us."

Lily smiled. "I am proud of this work. Every time I uncover a creative streak, I'm getting better. But with this, I finally believe that I am an artist. There's no doubt about that."

Ever since she was a child, she'd felt like an outcast, like she didn't belong in her own family. Though her mother had provided dance and art lessons, Lily later understood that these were only important in developing the characteristics she'd need to be a proper socialite. In the end, her mother had wanted her to focus on creating a successful marriage, just as her two older sisters had.

As for her father, he wanted her to do something useful with her life—more useful than creating art that no one wanted to buy. And apparently, spending her days volunteering as a docent at the art museum was more useful than creating art that no one wanted to buy. Or so he'd told her.

But her great-aunts had always encouraged her to dream big. They'd urged her to be patient, to keep working, to travel and absorb new cultures, to throw herself into life without any inhibitions or regrets. She'd trusted them, and now everything they'd told her was coming true.

"There's something else," Lily said softly, turning back to the painting. "I think I'm in love with him."

Violet laughed. "Of course you are, darling. It's all over that canvas. I might be a little bit in love with him myself."

"But what if he leaves?" Lily asked. "Or we fight? Will I stop painting like this?" She paused. "What if he doesn't love me?"

"Do you need him to love you?" Rose asked. "Sometimes it's easier to let them go when they don't love you back."

"Why would I want to let him go?" Lily asked.

"What if someone more interesting comes along?" Daisy asked with a coy smile.

Lily drew a deep breath. She'd taken romantic advice from her aunts before and had always thought it was reasonable. But the idea that she'd toss aside lovers for the rest of her life, one after the other, always looking for something better was...well, unsatisfying.

"Didn't you ever meet a man you wanted to spend

your entire life with?" she asked, directing the question at each one of them.

"I considered a few proposals in my time," Violet said, "but they never would have worked out. I didn't want to be a wife."

"I've always been quite happy on my own," Rose said. "It frightened me when I loved too deeply. I felt as if I'd lost control of my ability to reason. I prefer to run my own life."

"Personally, I think it stems from Father," offered Violet. "He was always such a bully with us. Trying to convince us to marry, threatening us with disinheritance. That's why he bought this place and built us each a cottage. Rather than us seeking our art in the world, he wanted us to bring it here to this place, where he could keep watch over his three rebellious daughters."

Lily ran her fingers over the ridges of paint, remembering how aroused Quinn's naked body had made her. Her hands had been trembling as she sketched and she'd felt a bit dizzy. There was no denying that at his touch she would almost instantly surrender.

She'd spent hours imagining what it might be like if they finally took that last step. They'd done almost everything else but had deliberately avoided crossing that line. When she finally did invite him inside her, she needed to know that she could let him go.

She'd have to make a decision sooner or later. The season was quickly coming to a close, and before long everyone would pack up and leave, giving room for the winter to move in and the snow to fall. The small woodstoves in the cabins and studios were enough to ward off the chill for now but they had no more than a month left.

"What are your plans for this winter?" Violet asked.

"I'm not sure," Lily replied. "I need to find a place to paint. Maybe Portugal. Or Spain. Someplace warm. Where are you going?"

"Why, we're staying here. Someone has to watch over this place, or they'll move in while we're gone and tear it all down."

"Well, it's decided. I'll spend the winter here, too," Lily said. "Which one of you is going to take me in and give me a room?"

Daisy looked at Rose and Rose glanced over at Violet. "I suppose we should tell her. We've been waiting all these years," said Violet.

Lily frowned. "Tell me what?"

"We want you to take Father's hunting cabin," Violet said, "and make it into a home for yourself. You should have a place of your own and we're happy to give it to you."

Lily had only been to the hunting cabin a few times over the years. When she rowed around the lake she could see the fieldstone building just offshore. Though it was secluded from the rest of the camp, it was closer to town and it had a functioning bathroom and winter insulation.

"Thank you. I could definitely be happy there," Lily said. "But it's a very dear gift."

"A dear gift for our dearest grandniece," Violet said, a tear in her eye. "It's quite selfish, actually. As Father wanted to keep us nearer, we want to keep you near."

Lily noticed that the sun was hanging low over the western horizon. "I should probably go," she said. "I promised Quinn I would help him sort through the property tax file."

"Have you found anything of interest?" Violet asked.

"Not yet." Lily sighed. "But I'm hopeful. Bernie has a lead on your father's secretary. If we find her, she might have some good information. But you need to keep looking. Now that you've given me my own cottage, I don't want it taken away."

Lily gave them each a kiss on the cheek, then picked up her painting and walked outside. She was walking back to her studio when she heard the loud rumble of an engine. She set her painting against a tree and ran down the path toward the dining hall. When she arrived she found an overnight delivery truck, the uniform driver chatting with Quinn.

The driver hopped back into the truck, made a quick U-turn, and sped out along the drive. She ran to Quinn's side and stared up at him.

"What is it?"

"Something from the lawyers," he murmured. A few seconds later, he forced a smile. "I'm starving. It's about time I take you to dinner."

"Are you asking me on a date?" Lily inquired.

Quinn chuckled softly. "Following tradition? That would be new. We should give it a try."

"And what about that ominous little package you're holding?"

Quinn glanced down at it, then handed it to Lily. "Open it up."

Lily considered his request for a long moment, then shook her head. "Nope. It can wait. I don't want anything to spoil our date."

He leaned close and dropped a kiss on her lips. "Good girl. I'm going to take a quick shower and put on some nice clothes and I'll meet you back here in a half hour. And make sure to wear shoes!"

Laughing, Lily skipped off down the path. "I'll wear shoes if you promise to shave off that scruff."

"And underwear!" Quinn shouted at her. "I don't want to be eating my salad and be distracted trying to see through your dress."

"I like flowers," she called to him.

TRISTAN WAS WAITING in his car, the top down, the radio playing a soft tune, when Lily wandered down the path. She waved at him as she approached and he immediately noticed that she hadn't followed his instructions. Though she was wearing a pretty new dress, it was obvious she wasn't wearing anything underneath.

Tristan hopped out of the car and circled around to the passenger side, then opened the door. He handed her a small bouquet of wildflowers as she sat down. Lily smiled, touching the flowers to her nose. He got back behind the wheel and turned on the ignition.

"Is there anyplace special you'd like to go?" he asked. "Maybe somewhere a little nicer than that road-house we went to last time?"

"There is a new place I've wanted to try," Lily said. "It's very quiet and out-of-the-way and we won't have to wait for a table. But we will have to bring our own pizza and wine."

"And where do we get pizza?"

"Just drive. I'll show you the way."

The sun had already set and there was a chill in the air, but it felt good to have the top down and enjoy the fresh smells of the woods. Tristan turned the music up, then reached over and slipped his hand around Lily's nape. Soft tendrils brushed against his skin and he pulled her closer and kissed her temple.

"We've spent so much time at camp it feels strange to get away. Almost like we're sneaking out."

"It's probably for the best," Lily said. "I heard that tonight will be the last skinny-dipping party. At least we'll avoid that invitation."

"Oh, no. I was really hoping to participate, at least once."

"The aunts would have been pleased. They saw my painting and were very curious about the frontal view."

Tristan cursed beneath his breath. "You showed it to them?"

"Of course I did. We always share our work. The rest of the camp will see it soon enough." She glanced over at him. "What? Don't you think it's good?"

"I do. Although, I'm not sure I'm a good judge. Or even a good model. Are you going to sell it?"

Lily shrugged. "I'm not sure. Are you interested in buying?"

"Maybe," Tristan said, "or maybe I'd be interested in a portrait of you."

"If you want a naked picture of me," Lily said, "you

just have to pull out your phone and snap one. It would be much more realistic."

Tristan had spent so much time with Lily that he had grown used to her audacious wit but there were still moments when she surprised him. He loved that they could say anything to each other. And though there were still secrets between them, they didn't seem to make as much difference anymore.

Lily directed him to a small roadside diner where a neon sign assured visitors that they served pizza. They walked inside and sat down at the bar, ordered a large pizza to go and enjoyed a glass of wine while they waited. Lily told him about the next painting she wanted to do, explaining that if he exposed all his bits and pieces, she would make him look good.

Tristan was amazed at how much fun they were having together. Being out in public seemed to energize Lily and she flirted and seemed intent on making him laugh. It was as if all her worries about the camp and her aunts were left behind.

The bartender brought them their pizza and Tristan purchased a bottle of wine before they walked out into the chilly night air. He put up the convertible top before they drove out of the parking lot and to his surprise Lily pointed him back in the direction they had come.

"It's kind of tricky to find," she explained, "especially in the dark." When they came to a curve in the road, she had him slow down. Then when they reached the next intersection she realized they'd gone too far and had him turn around.

"It's here somewhere," she said. "Slower."

Tristan stared into the darkness at the edge of the road, wondering how anyone could find a turn amid the thick woods and black sky. But finally Lily yelled "Stop," and pointed to two narrow ruts with nothing but an old fence post and a horseshoe to mark the entrance.

"What is this place?"

"It used to belong to my great-grandfather," Lily said. "But now it belongs to me. My aunts gave it to me this afternoon. I'm going to live here this winter."

"Out in the middle of the woods? All alone?"

"My aunts will be nearby. Just across the lake. We thought it would be best to stay in case the lawsuit carries on."

The path through the woods grew wider as they approached the shore of the lake. Finally, the woods gave way to a wide clearing. The headlights illuminated a low stone cottage, wide rafters holding up a wood shingled roof, and a picturesque porch surrounding the cottage on three sides. Lily sighed, and Tristan glanced over at her.

"It's beautiful," he said.

"I know." She opened the car door and stepped out. "I can't remember what it's like inside. The aunts have kept it up, so it should be nice."

They walked together up the front porch steps. When they got to the door, Lily went to the front porch post and pulled out a small block of wood at the base. The spot held an old key and she slipped into the door and released the creaky lock.

Unlike most of the cabins at the colony, this cottage had electricity, and the moment Lily flipped a switch, the rustic interior came to light. They both wandered around, taking in the details, from the stone fireplace and hearth, to the multi-paned windows. The decor was dated and very masculine, but to Tristan's surprise, the place was tidy without a musty smell at all.

"This is great," he said, crossing to examine a rack of old fishing poles. A velvet-covered frame displayed a selection of hand-tied flies and another cabinet held a rack of old hunting rifles and shotguns. "Do you know when the cabin was built?"

"Sometime in the thirties, I think. My great-great-grandfather bought the land during the depression. He built this first and then the three cottages for my aunts when they were in their early twenties. That would have been in about the late sixties."

"Why don't you try to find a corkscrew. I'll light a fire, then we can have our dinner."

"I can't believe this is mine," she said.

Tristan watched as she wandered around the cabin, taking in all the details. Most women would find the cottage too rough and masculine, but Lily apparently saw the place as an extension of a family she loved. He realized that in her eyes, it was perfect.

She walked to a set of doors that overlooked the lake and she stood silently, peering out into the darkness. "We can't lose this," she said, turning to him. Tears glittered in her eyes. "Promise me we won't."

He crossed the room and drew her into his arms, kissing her eyes and cheeks, the moisture from her tears making his lips damp.

Lily wrapped her arms around his neck, returning his kiss with fierce determination. She pulled him along to the sofa, her lips still locked to his, and dragged him down until she could curl up in his lap. Tristan furrowed his fingers through her windswept hair, molding her mouth to his until the kiss became deep and urgent.

As they continued to kiss, Tristan stretched out on top of her, his hips pressed firmly against hers. Tristan gripped her wrists and pulled them above her head, trailing kisses along the curve of her neck.

Lily arched her back. "Make love to me," she murmured. Her tongue traced the crease in his lips and he groaned as he opened to another kiss.

His palms slid along her torso until they cupped her breasts. He nuzzled the soft flesh, then teased at her nipples with his teeth and tongue.

Lily wriggled out from beneath him and stood beside the sofa. She reached for the hem of her dress and slowly tugged it up along her thighs.

His hands dropped to hers, his fingers clasping her wrists. "Let me do that," he said. Tristan sat up, then grabbed her hem in his fists, drawing the fabric up, inch by inch, along her calves and then her thighs.

As he revealed naked skin, he pressed his lips to carefully chosen spots—the curve of her calf, the soft skin behind her knee, the warm flesh on the inside of her thigh. Lily moaned softly, urging him on, her fingers tangled in his hair.

When he finally found the damp spot between her thighs, her breath caught in her throat and she cried out, as if the touch of his tongue sent a shock through her body. He felt her tremble, and in that moment, all his doubts and fears melted away

This was how it would always be between them—this crazy, undeniable desire. And the little lies and the tiny deceptions would be nothing against this passion. Passion would always win out.

But for Tristan, wanting Lily came with a whole host of risks. She took a casual attitude toward sex, as if she could easily disconnect passion from emotion. But the more time he spent with her, the more Tristan realized his feelings for her ran deeper than just desire.

He wanted to make her happy, to protect her, to show her that having a man in her life didn't mean she was weak or conventional. These feelings surprised him, and at first, he thought they'd be easy to ignore. But in reality, they were growing stronger with every day that passed.

Tristan remembered how he'd chided his brother Thom when he'd announced he'd fallen in love. Then, it had seemed impossible for Tristan to ever be in the same situation. He'd felt that something so complicated as falling in love would probably destroy itself before it was fully realized. But now Tristan realized that a guy couldn't always see these things coming.

Like a huge, silent, invisible freight train, love was barreling down the track on a collision course with Tristan's heart. There had been a time in his life when he would have jumped off the track and avoided the impact. But now here he was, watching the train approach and wondering how good it might feel to get knocked off his feet.

6

THE MOMENT HE touched her, Lily was lost. Every time they shared an intimate moment, her ability to resist him seemed to diminish. She didn't want to need him, to spend every moment of her day thinking about when they'd be together again, but she couldn't help herself.

She'd always been far too independent to allow a man—or his touch—to rule her life. But here she was, begging him to seduce her, willing to trust a man she barely knew and to believe in a man she thought she might love.

Still clutching the fabric of her skirt, Tristan drew his tongue along the soft folds that hid her sex. Gently, he nudged her legs apart until he had complete access. For Lily, the waiting was almost unbearable and she finally reached down and guided him to the precise spot.

Waves of pleasure washed over her as his tongue teased. He knew exactly how to bring her closer to the edge. But he wasn't in a hurry. Every time Lily felt herself begin to lose control, he slowed his pace. It was a delicious, provocative dance between the two of them, the rhythms of her body increasing as they neared the climax of the music.

When she felt as if her legs were about to collapse beneath her, he pulled her down on the sofa. Impatient with his teasing, Lily whispered her need, begging him to take her the rest of the way, arching against him until he finally relented.

In the end, her orgasm overwhelmed her, exploding through her body like a shower of sparks, setting every nerve on fire until her skin was flushed and her breath came in gasps.

Spasms shook her body, leaving her weak and sated. Tristan crawled alongside her and pulled her against his body as the last of her shudders dissolved.

Lily held tight to the front of his shirt until her breathing slowed, then glanced up at him. The boyish grin returned and he dropped a kiss onto her damp lips.

Her gaze fixed on his shirt, open at the front. She hadn't remembered undoing the buttons but she must have. He had a way of distracting her from fulfilling his needs. But she wasn't going to allow it this time.

Lily pushed him into the cushions as she straddled his lap, tossing the blanket aside. "I'm not cold," she whispered. To prove her point, she reached for the hem of her dress and drew it up along her body.

Quinn groaned softly as his gaze skimmed over her naked flesh. Lily smiled as she reached out and undid the rest of his buttons. She brushed the soft fabric of his shirt aside, leaning in to press her lips to the center of his chest. "You have too many clothes on," she said.

"We could do something about that," he replied.

"Show me," she said.

He stood, then pulled her to her feet, taking a short break to indulge in a long, deep kiss. His hands moved across her body, now unimpeded by clothing, to her breasts, to her hips, to her backside.

She'd seen him naked before, even touched him. But this was different. This time, it would live up to all her fantasies. "Go ahead," she said. "Take off your clothes. You can start with your shirt."

"I like it when you take charge," Quinn said.

"Then after you're done with the shirt, you can start on your jeans."

He dutifully stripped out of his clothes and when he was finished, Lily slowly circled him, taking in his masculine beauty with an artist's eye. It had been difficult when she'd sketched him to look at his naked body without getting aroused, but now she could allow herself that luxury.

Skimming her fingertips over his flesh, she searched for her favorite spots: the sharp slash of muscle that defined his hips and belly...the wide expanse of his shoulders...the trail of hair that traced a path from his chest to his waist and beyond. "You have the most amazing body," she murmured.

Lily stepped in front of him, then reached out and wrapped her fingers around his hard shaft. A groan rumbled in his chest, but when she dropped to her knees and took him into the warmth of her mouth, he gasped her name.

She wanted to prove that she could control his desire as easily as he controlled hers. She needed them to be equals in this relationship, the power to seduce balanced perfectly between them. She didn't want to feel weak at his touch, she only wanted his caress to fuel her need.

His fingers tangled in her hair and she allowed him to control the pace when it suited her. And when it didn't, Lily used her tongue to draw him closer to the edge. But she had other plans for them both, and when he was just a heartbeat from release, Lily slowly rose, turning her back to him and reaching behind her to grab his hips.

"Are you sure you want this?" he murmured, his breath warm against her ear.

"I've wanted this since the day I met you," Lily said. "I'm just not sure what's taken us so long."

She turned in his arms, then pulled him down onto the sofa. He settled himself between her legs, drawing her thighs up along his hips. Just feeling the weight of his body on hers was enough to make her pulse quicken. His mouth came down on hers and he kissed her, his tongue delving deep, as if he were desperate to taste her desire as well as hear it and see it.

His hips moved against hers as his shaft slid against her core. She shifted beneath him, tempting him to slip inside her. But he stopped suddenly, then stretched out to grab his jeans from the floor.

Quinn pulled a condom from his wallet and held it up. "We only have one of these. So we're going to have to ration it."

Lily giggled. "Not a chance." She grabbed the package and tore it open, then deftly sheathed him. His breath caught in his throat as she smoothed the latex over his erection, as if her touch was enough to steal his control. "There," she said. "Now you're ready."

"And are you?" he asked, his gaze meeting hers.

"Definitely."

Lily smiled as he slowly pushed inside her, each inch creating a new level of pleasure until he was buried deep inside her. The moment he began to move, she let her body drift free, focusing on the pulsing need that seemed to have taken control.

Lily focused only on the sensations coursing through her, the warmth of his skin against hers, the taste of his tongue and the soft rhythm of his gasps as he drove deeper and deeper inside of her.

She didn't feel the orgasm coming until it was almost upon her. He increased his pace and shifted above her. Suddenly each thrust sent a current through her body, building and building the pressure until every nerve in her body tingled.

Lily moaned softly, pressing her face into his shoulder and focusing on the wave of feeling rushing over her. A deep spasm rocked her body and she let go, surrendering completely to her body's instincts.

She cried out as her fingers clutched at his shoulders. Lily felt his muscles tense and then he joined her, driving deep before losing himself to his own orgasm.

He rolled to her side, completely exhausted and spent. Lily moaned. "Oh, my," she murmured. "I didn't expect that."

"Yours? Or mine?"

"Mine," she said. "It usually doesn't happen that way."

"It usually doesn't feel that way for me," he said.

"Should we do it again and see if it works the same way?" Lily asked.

"Maybe we could relax for three or four minutes," he suggested. "We have wine and a cold pizza. I could build that fire."

"I *am* hungry, come to think of it," Lily said, her stomach growling as she spoke. "And it's getting chilly. I'll take care of the food and drink. You make the fire and we'll meet back here."

They didn't bother with clothes. In truth, she and Quinn had always been more comfortable naked. Lily grabbed the pizza and wine and set it down on the floor in front of the fireplace. As she wandered back to the kitchen, she opened one of the doors that overlooked the lake.

A soft rain had begun to fall. She stepped off the porch onto a stone walkway that led down to the water. The rain spattered against her warm skin and she angled her face up to the sky, enjoying the impromptu shower.

Lily felt Quinn's arms circle her waist and she leaned back against him. "Smell that? It's the smell of green." She turned in his arms. "Let's go for a swim. I love to swim in the rain."

"You're not cold?" he asked.

"No," she said, starting down the stone path. "Come on. It's been a while since I've checked out the beach here."

They walked together, hand in hand, to the water, then waded in until they were up to their chins. "I like this place. It's peaceful."

"You don't want to go back to the colony?"

She shook his head. "Let's spend the night here. It will be nice to have a little privacy." She stared across the water in the direction of the colony. She could make out the two boat docks and part of the dining hall, but the rest of the buildings were hidden by the trees.

"Do you really think we can save it for them?" Lily asked.

"We're going to try," Quinn said. "We won't leave any stone unturned."

Lily's emotions overwhelmed her once again and she hugged him close. "Thank you." For the first time since meeting him, she felt entirely at ease. She knew exactly who he was and what he wanted. They weren't strangers anymore. They were friends and lovers. Who knew what else was possible?

THEY TOSSED CUSHIONS and pillows on the old braided rug, then found faded quilts to spread on top of them. Tristan curled against her body, his chin resting on her shoulder as they both watched the glowing embers of the fire. Life seemed almost perfect here with her.

"The summer is too short," Lily murmured. "It's Labor Day this weekend. After that, there's nothing left." She pulled his arms tighter around her body. "I don't want it to end."

"It doesn't have to end," Tristan said. "If you're staying here for the winter, we can see plenty of each other.

You'll need someone to chop wood and fetch supplies and build fires."

"Would you live here with me?" she asked.

The question took him by surprise. Tristan had never once considered living with a woman. But now it seemed like the perfect solution. He could continue working on her case. He could try to decide what he wanted to do for the rest of his life, maybe look into starting a firm of his own that focused on helping real people instead of just people with money. And, he could spend more time with Lily.

Hell, he wasn't even worried about the implications of moving in together. All he cared about was falling asleep beside Lily every night and waking up with her every morning. Hot or cold, rain or shine, rich or poor, he could imagine himself happy just to have each day as a brand-new adventure.

And yet, he couldn't ignore the lies that still stood between them. Hell, she didn't even know his real name. But then, he could remedy that right now.

"Remember how I told you that Quinn James was my pen name?"

She gave him an odd look. "No, I don't remember you saying that. I thought Quinn James was your real name."

"It isn't," he said.

Lily drew a deep breath, let it out. "Bernie isn't actually Bernie," she said. "His real name is Todd. And Raymond Finch is really Harold Fincher. What is your real name?"

A long silence spun out between them and Tristan held his breath. "Tristan," he said. "Tristan Quinn."

Tristan waited, wondering if she might have seen or heard his name before. It was on the letterhead for his law firm, but people rarely read the list of lawyers as it was printed in tiny letters down the left side of legal stationary.

"Tristan," she said. "That's a nice name. Why would you want to change it?"

"It's…odd," he said.

"Do you mind that I just call you Quinn?" Lily asked.

"No," he replied. But that wasn't the truth. He looked forward to the day when he heard his name on her lips, or when, in the throes of passion, she would whisper it, or perhaps in the midst of sleep. "But you might try 'Tristan.'"

"Tristan," she said. "I think it makes a better pen name."

"For romance novels," he said. "Or fantasy novels. Not for legal thrillers." He'd reveal the truth about the book after he'd proved himself as a lawyer.

"Tristan," she repeated softly.

"Lily," he replied.

"Tristan."

"Lily." Tristan leaned forward and brushed a kiss across her lips. "So tell me something I don't know about you. Tell me a secret. Tell me a story."

He listened as she recounted a story about visiting a marketplace in Morocco. Lily was good at painting with acrylics and oils and watercolors. But her ability to paint with words took his breath away. He closed his eyes and his mind filled with colorful images of a strange and exotic place.

Tristan couldn't help but feel a measure of regret that he'd never be able to offer her the luxuries and adventures she'd become accustomed to in her life. He often found himself thinking about a future with Lily, but if they didn't win the case for the colony, where would they live? With his career currently in shambles, there was very little he could offer anyone, much less a wealthy heiress. And he wasn't sure he could accept living off her money.

Lost in his own dilemma, Tristan stared into the fire and silence fell between them.

"I can't imagine losing the colony," Lily said finally. "It would kill me if I let that happen to the aunts. This is their life. And it's mine, too. For me, this will always be home. My parents' big stone mansion never felt like that." She slowly ran her fingers up and down his arm and Tristan could tell she was deep in thought.

The colony and the artists staying there had formed the person Lily was today—kind, compassionate, open-minded, spontaneous. He wanted more than anything to win the case for her.

"What are you thinking?"

"I wonder if we should get more radical. More aggresive. We can't afford to just sit back and let them run the show."

"We are not getting bullets for the guns," Tristan warned.

"They're mostly prop guns," she said. "But I have something else in mind."

He waited, sensing that he was going to disapprove of her idea.

Lily took a deep breath. "Let's get arrested. I'd love to see a photo of all of us behind bars. Or better yet, once we are in jail, we could go on a hunger strike. Can you imagine? The media would play attention to that."

"That seems a bit drastic," Tristan said. "After all, your comrades-in-arms are senior citizens."

"All right, then I'll do the hunger strike on my own." She paused. "I've never been in jail," Lily murmured. "I mean, I've stood up for a lot of different causes over the years. I've protested and demonstrated. I've even been pepper-sprayed. But I've never actually been arrested."

She glanced at Tristan, taking in the worried expression on his face. "What about you? Have you ever been in jail?"

"I've never done any protesting," he said. "But I've been incarcerated several times."

"For what?" Lily seemed shocked by his admission.

"Once for stealing a car. Another few times for petty theft."

"You're a criminal?" Lily asked.

"I was a juvenile delinquent," Tristan explained. "I had a dysfunctional childhood."

Lily shook her head. He was trying to be casual about it, but he could see she was curious about this side of him, new to her. "Do you mind talking about it?" she asked.

He glanced around the empty room. "It's just a really depressing story and I don't really like to bring it up."

"Then start with your family," she said.

"I had a great family for a few years. Two younger brothers. My dad was an Irish immigrant. A real character. Big drinker. The life of the party. The friendliest guy you'd ever meet. He'd give you the shirt off his back if you asked. Because of the drinking he had a hard time keeping a job, but he always seemed to find a way to pay the bills. Until he was killed trying to rob a gas station. And then we went from happy to homeless."

"Oh, no," Lily murmured. She turned over to face him, reaching up to touch his face.

"My mother started to drink heavily to cope with the stress, and then she couldn't hold a job herself. Then came the drugs. Taking them, selling them. Me and my two brothers were left to raise ourselves."

"You seem to have done a fine job of it," Lily offered.

"My mother ended up in prison. My brothers and I probably would have ended up there, too, if my grandmother hadn't stepped in at the last minute." He looked down at Lily, meeting her gaze. "Too much information?"

"I guess I sound pretty silly complaining about my own childhood, then," Lily murmured. "Swiss boarding schools and summers with my aunts."

"We both had our challenges and we both made it

out the other side," Tristan said. "Isn't that what really matters? Look at us. We're functioning adults."

Lily nodded, then reached out and took his hand, lacing her fingers through his. He slipped his arm around her shoulders and pulled her close, kissing the top of her head.

"Can we stay here forever?" she murmured.

"No," Tristan said. "But we can keep coming back."

"Are you sorry you got pulled into this?" Lily asked.

Tristan hooked his finger beneath her chin and turned her gaze up to his. He bent close and brushed his lips across hers. "I'm not. I see how much the colony means to you and your aunts. It means a lot to me, too."

Tristan wanted to tell her about the notice, the one that that been delivered that afternoon. But he decided to wait until the morning. She'd just worry about it all night long. And now that they'd found some privacy, he had other plans for their time together.

LILY PACED BACK and forth in front of the dining hall. A crowd had gathered there in response to Tristan's bell. He held the FedEx package in his hand.

"Why didn't you tell us sooner?" Finch shouted.

"I suppose I could have," he said. "But there wasn't much we could do about it."

"We can follow Lily's plan. It's time to be more pro-active," Finch said.

"We were proactive yesterday," Tristan said. "We built a gate at the end of the drive, put a lock on it, and posted No Trespassing signs. Today, all we can do is find out what they want."

"What if they try to come in?"

"They won't. They don't want trouble. In the meantime, we need to continue going through the papers and ledgers. We still haven't pinned down the date when the sisters started paying the property taxes on this place. That's a very important piece of information."

Lily glanced around the crowd. "Has anyone found something that might help our case?" She scanned the faces that watched her, disappointment overwhelming her. She drew a ragged breath. "I think we need to go to Plan B. Arrest and hunger strike."

"Lily, the notice is just for a preliminary meeting. I'm not letting them on the property. I'll talk with them out on the road, or we'll go to town. I won't let them in here. And I don't want you or anyone else to come out. Understood?"

Everyone reluctantly nodded. He turned to the sisters, who stood on the porch like a trio of songbirds, dressed in brilliant colors and flowing silk scarves. "Promise?" he asked.

The three of them gave their assent. Lily observed them shrewdly. She could tell when they were lying and she suspected they were formulating their own plans as Tristan spoke. Though she trusted Tristan to represent their interests, she couldn't forget that until yesterday, she hadn't even known his real name.

Besides, there was a difference between trusting a man with her body and trusting him with her life. She could always handle a few regrets when it came to a love affair gone bad, but not the recriminations she'd feel over a ruined future.

"Are you sure you should be going on your own?" Lily said, drawing Tristan away. "Shouldn't you have a—a witness there?"

"If I could guarantee that anyone I brought with me would stand silently and not comment on anything, I'd be fine. But you know that won't happen. Lily, there's going to be a lot of things said that you shouldn't hear. We need to keep everyone positive and not worrying over little details. Can you do that?"

Lily drew a deep breath, then nodded. "All right."

He rejoined the group. "Bernie, how are you doing on the secretary search?"

"A couple of former coworkers said she went to California to live with a sister. I'm making a lot of calls, but nothing yet."

"Get someone to help you," Tristan said. "We're running out of time." To Lily he said, "I'm going to go out and wait for the lawyers. You keep things calm back here, all right?"

Lily nodded, then pushed up on her toes and gave him a quick kiss. "Good luck." She walked down to his car and closed the door after he slid in behind the wheel. "I'll see you later."

He grinned at her. "No, I'll see you later. All of you." He gave her a wink, then threw the car into gear and headed out toward the road. Lily wandered over to her aunts, who had decided to enjoy a pitcher of lemonade that someone had brought out from the kitchen.

"Pull up a chair, dear," Violet said. "You might as well relax and let Quinn do his work."

"Tristan," Lily said. "His first name is Tristan. His last name is Quinn."

"Tristan Quinn?" Rose asked. "Why does that name sound familiar?"

"Tristan and Iseult. The Arthurian legend."

"Wasn't that Tristram?" Rose asked.

"It's spelled several ways. They were star-crossed lovers from warring clans. You and I saw the Wagner opera when we were in Bayreuth the summer of 1964. Don't you remember?" Daisy asked. "There it was Tristan and Isolde."

"Yes. But that's not it." Rose shook her head. "Sometimes I feel as if my brain is made of feathers. A good wind and all my memories will just blow away."

Violet chuckled. "Just plug your ears, dear, and you'll be fine."

Rose gave her sister a playful slap, giggling as she did. Then she stopped suddenly, an odd expression coming over her face. "Excuse me for a moment." She got up from the table and walked inside the dining hall, the screen door slamming behind her.

Lily plopped down on her chair and reached for a fresh paper cup. She poured herself some lemonade and took a sip. "I stayed at the hunting cottage last night," she said. "And the night before."

"Did you?" Violet said. "I love that place. I remember all the good days with Father when I'm there."

"I looked around and I didn't find any papers. The desk was empty."

"We cleaned it all up after he passed. We thought he might have had a safe but we were never able to find it."

Daisy piped up. "I don't know how you can have such good memories of that place, Vi. All I remember are the terrible rows we had, the three of us on one side and Father on the other."

"I do remember a few of those arguments," Violet said.

"I remember one. It was right after my twenty-first birthday. The three of us had been in New York City. We stayed at the Ritz and we went out to all the popular clubs—the Copa, the Stork Club, we even went to the Cotton Club."

"We ended up at some pretty disreputable places," Violet continued. "Places that were off limits to proper young ladies but where they had the best acts. Anyway, the three of us spent the night with some Brazilian diplomats who kept buying us champagne cocktails. We ended up drinking ourselves silly and dancing on the bar in our garters, brassieres and petticoats. It was fabulous."

"And it was in the papers," Daisy said. "When we got home for the holidays, we all came here and Father summoned us to the cottage. He was furious."

"He kept waving these papers at us. Telling us we couldn't be trusted to run our own lives. I thought he was talking about our trust, about giving us control of the money. But what if he was talking about the property? The lake and the three cottages he built for us? What if that paper was the deed?"

Lily leaned forward. "Did you see what was on the paper?"

"No," Violet said.

Daisy shook her head. "No. But it wouldn't make sense that it was our trust money. That came to each of us when we turned twenty-five, so at that point only Violet would have been affected. And she got her money right on time."

"I have to tell Tristan," Lily said.

"It can wait until he gets back," Violet said.

"It can't wait! There's a piece of paper out there stating your father intended to give you three this property."

"Darling, that's only a guess at what he was talking about," Daisy warned. "It was so many years ago."

At that moment, Rose came bursting out of the dining hall door, a piece of paper clutched in her hand. She hurried over to the table and Lily quickly stood so her aunt could sit down.

"I knew I recognized the name Tristan Quinn. Oh, cad! Rogue! Scoundrel!"

Lily took the sheet and scanned the text. It was a letter from the legal firm representing the family foundation— a letter from the enemy. "What's the problem?"

Rose pointed in the general direction of a list of lawyers down the right hand side of the page. Lily skimmed the list, her gaze stopping when it came to Tristan Quinn. "Jerk. Creep. Asshole!" she muttered.

"Lily!" Violet cried.

"Look," Lily said. "Here he is. Tristan Quinn. He works for the enemy. I let a snake into our camp. And now he's out there negotiating *on our behalf* with his own firm."

With a low curse, Lily strode into the dining hall

and went right for the gun cabinet. She removed the most realistic-looking rifle and threw the strap over her shoulder, then headed back out to the porch.

"Lily, what are you doing?" Violet hurried up to her and grabbed her arm. "Stop this."

"That's exactly what I'm going to do. I'm going to stop this ridiculous charade and chase Tristan Quinn out of camp."

The earlier crowd of residents had dispersed back to their cabins and their midmorning tasks. But a few remained and when they saw her distress, they came running. But before they could follow her, she took off at a jog down the driveway and out to the road. As she ran, Lily had plenty of time to figure out exactly what she planned to say to him. But then she heard his voice and her emotions got the better of her.

Why had he lied to her? Did he believe she was so naive that he could waltz into camp and fool her forever? Lily wanted answers and she intended to get them. And then she'd send him away for good.

7

"WHAT THE HELL are you doing, Quinn? We sent you to do a job, then you tell us you quit and now you say you're working for these loonies?"

Tristan stared across the gate at his former boss, Reggie Dunlap. His former paralegal, Melanie Parker, was also part of the contingent, like Stanley coming to the jungle to rescue Dr. Livingstone.

"I don't need to be rescued," Tristan said.

"You're in line for a damned partnership, Quinn, and you're going to throw the whole thing away to stand behind this group of wackos?"

"They're not wackos, Reggie. They're a community. A family. And you can't come in here and try to take it all away just because you can."

"Your friends have had every chance to prove ownership of this property. I haven't seen a single document that backs up that claim. They're squatters and have been for years."

"Liar!" The voice came from behind him and Tristan

spun around to see Lily approaching, a rifle clutched in her hands.

"You're a liar! And—and a snake. A liar and a snake!"

The sheriff held up his hands. "Don't worry, it's not loaded."

The photographer from the local paper stepped forward to take a few snaps. "Lily, can I quote you on that?"

"Absolutely!" Lily said.

"Who were you directing that comment to?"

"Tristan Quinn," she said.

"But isn't he your lawyer?"

"Not anymore," Lily said. She strode up to Tristan and gave him a shove. "Get out."

"Quinn, what the hell is going on?" Dunlap said.

"You're fired," Lily said. "Just get out now." She drew a ragged breath. "You're a lawyer for the enemy. How long were you going to keep that a secret?"

"I'm not," Tristan said. "I resigned a couple days ago. Yes, the firm sent me here to negotiate a settlement, but once I saw this place and I met you and your aunts, I couldn't do it."

"It's all been a lie."

"No," Tristan said. "Most of it has been real. So real and wonderful that the lies didn't seem to make a difference."

"They make a difference to me!" she shouted.

"How can they make a difference to you, Lily? You never once said you wanted anything more than sex.

No strings, remember? Or did your feelings change along the way? Mine certainly did."

He noticed tears swimming in her eyes and he reached out to touch her, but she shook her head. "Please leave."

"I can't."

"We'll find a different lawyer. We don't need you."

"You do need me," he murmured, leaning close. "And I need you."

"No!" Lily fumbled with the gun, using it like a club, holding it between them as she stepped back.

"Put the gun down, Lily. You're not going to hit me." Tristan reached for the old rifle, but instead of letting him take it, Lily swung it at him and then let it go. Tristan watched it sail through the air. The moment it hit a tree, it discharged, the shot ringing through the silent woods.

The sound threw everyone into action. Dunlap hurried for the cover of his car. Melanie quickly followed him. The photographer squatted behind a tree and began to furiously snap photos. The sheriff pulled his own firearm.

"All right, folks," the sheriff. "I want y'all to freeze!"

"Oh, shit," Tristan muttered.

He quickly grabbed Lily and forced her behind his back, putting his body between her and the sheriff. However, the sheriff and his deputy were determined to control the situation and they'd already started coming toward them, guns drawn. Lily scampered out from behind him, but the deputy caught her, twisting her arm until she stopped moving. "Oww! Let me go," Lily cried as they put her in handcuffs. "You're hurting me."

"Release my client!" Tristan called. "There's no reason to arrest her."

"She discharged a gun within town limits," the sheriff said.

Lily slapped the deputy over the head, knocking his hat to the ground. When he let go of Lily's arm, Tristan grabbed it. Between warnings from the sheriff and the deputy and Lily's colorful cursing, Tristan accidentally elbowed the sheriff in the nose.

"Enough!" the sheriff said. "Get these two in the cruiser. They're both under arrest. The rest of you get out of here. I've had it with this situation. You're either going to take this to a proper court or you're going to have your meetings elsewhere. Now shoo!"

Five minutes later, Tristan was sitting in the backseat of the deputy's squad car, Lily beside him. "Don't say anything," he murmured. "Just let me do the talking."

"Why would I do that?" Lily asked.

"I don't know," Tristan whispered. "Maybe because I'm a lawyer and I can keep you out of serious trouble. Did you realize that gun was loaded?"

"No," she replied in a soft voice. "We use it as a prop gun. It was probably a blank."

"They're going to separate us," he said. "When they try to interview you, just tell them you want your lawyer and have them come and get me. Remember, don't say anything until we have a chance to talk alone."

They rode the rest of the way to town in silence,

Lily staring out the window at the passing scenery and Tristan hoping she might turn and look at him. He knew she was angry, and she had every reason to be upset. But the fact was he'd switched sides long ago.

He thought back over their time together, trying to pinpoint the moment when he'd fallen for her. Was it that first kiss that they'd shared? Or was it when he'd found her standing in the road, barely dressed, her naked body moving gracefully beneath a nearly sheer dress? By the time they'd finally made love at the stone cottage, he'd been certain that he didn't want anyone else in the world.

Sheriff Larson and his deputy led them both inside the station. Tristan hoped that they'd be put in the same cell and he'd have a chance to talk to Lily privately, but he was left alone in a holding cell and she was whisked away to another location.

Tristan waited, glancing at his watch as he paced the width of his cell. As each minute passed, he grew more impatient—and more worried about Lily. She was so naive in many ways and he imagined the sheriff bullying her and forcing her to admit to something she didn't do.

An hour passed and Tristan walked to the cell door and grabbed the bars. "Hey! Is anyone out there? I'm supposed to get a phone call. I want my phone call! I want to talk to my client. You can't speak to Lily Harrison without me being present."

A few moments later, Sheriff Larson sauntered in, his keys jingling as he walked. "What are you howling about?"

"I've been beyond patient," Tristan said. "Where is Lily? Why am I still here?"

The sheriff chuckled. "She's long gone. Someone paid her fine and took her home an hour ago."

Tristan bit back a curse. Now he might never have a chance to talk to her. "Why am I still sitting here?"

"Well, I hadn't quite decided what to do about you. You seem to be the cause of this whole kerfuffle."

"Kerfuffle? And I suppose you have a law against kerfuffles?"

"Don't you get smart with me, sonny. Seems you've been doing a lot of storytelling recently."

"All right. I did work for the firm representing the family foundation and I came up here to try to negotiate a settlement before the family takes more aggressive action. I thought if I got to know the key players, I might be more effective." He paused. "After I met Lily, I just kind of lost track of what I was supposed to do."

"Well, I can understand that. She's a pretty young thing. If I were thirty years younger, I'd be calling on her myself."

"Of course. I should have been up-front with her from the start." A sick feeling twisted the pit of his stomach. She'd never forgive him. He should have told her the truth from the start and taken his chances. Now there was no going back. "Are you going to charge me? If you are, then let's get on with it."

"I might be persuaded to let you go without a charge if you promise to drive directly out of town and never come back to this area again."

"I can't promise that," Tristan said. "I have some unfinished business with the Pigglestone sisters."

"Then I think I'll give you a little more time to think about things." He started toward the door.

Tristan cursed softly. "All right. All right. But I will need to get my car. And that's at the colony."

Sheriff Larson reached out and unlocked the cell door, then swung it open. "It's still parked on the road according to my deputy. Your coworker can drive you over. But that's it. Pick up the car and head out of town."

"Coworker?"

"She arrived a little while ago," the sheriff said. "Melanie Parker? She paid your fine. I'd recommend you both get out of town as quickly as possible."

Tristan strode down the hall, then turned at the sign that indicated the lobby. But as he pushed open the door, Tristan had only one goal. To find Lily and explain everything to her.

"Tristan!"

Melanie Parker jumped to her feet from the chair she was sitting in and hustled across the lobby. "Are you all right?"

"Yes, thank you, Melanie. And thank you for taking care of the fine. I'll pay you back. But right now I need to you drive me to the colony to get my car. Then I have to find Lily. And you should get back to work. Don't give them an excuse to fire you."

She trailed after him as he walked outside. "They don't need one. I quit," she said.

Tristan spun around. "You what?"

"I quit. You were the only reason I stayed. You were the only guy worth working for." She paused. "I—I don't mean that in any kind of romantic way. It's just that you were the one guy in the whole firm who did pro bono work, and I found that admirable. That and you're always nice to me."

Tristan wasn't sure what to stay. "What are you going to do for money?"

"I've been saving. I want to write full-time. I have enough money to last for a year. So that's how long I have to sell my book."

"It may not take that long. The guys in critique group love your book," he said. "After you take me there, you should go introduce yourself around camp. It's only right that they know the real author of the manuscript they've been reading."

"Would you introduce me?" Melanie asked.

"I may not be welcome there anymore."

Tristan got into Melanie's car and showed her the way. As they drove, his thoughts returned to Lily. What would happen if he barged back into camp? They all knew him and some of them trusted him. He would explain what had happened and assure them that he was going to continue helping them. The fight was not over.

"I'd still like to help you."

"I expect you'll be too busy. According to some of the writers at the colony, you have a very promising career as an author in front of you."

"I—I do?"

"After you drop me off, go into camp and tell them

I sent you to pick up my things. Ask for Finch and introduce yourself. He loved your book."

"Raymond Finch?" she asked.

"I think that's his first name. He used to write crime novels, but now he's working on his memoirs."

"My father loved his novels," Melanie said. "He used to read them to me when I was a kid. He liked my book? *Raymond Finch* actually *liked* my book?"

"Yes, and he could tell that I hadn't written it," Tristan said.

"What exactly did he say?"

"I can't remember—not exactly. You can ask him yourself."

"Who else was in the critique group?"

"I don't remember a lot of the names. Bernie Wilson. He writes some kind of—"

"Sci-fi. Bernard Wilson. I love him. I've read all his books. Is he working on another in his Knights of Neyshar series? Oh my God, I would love to talk to him about his work. I could ask him about his character arcs…"

Tristan listened distractedly as Melanie chattered on about Bernie's books, recounting her favorite plots and characters. His own thoughts were firmly fixed on his next move with Lily. He'd get his car, then check into a local motel and wait until night. After dark, he'd have no trouble sneaking into camp and into her cabin to talk to her.

He had to find a way to apologize first, to find the words to express how desperate he'd been to get to know her. Once she learned he'd quit his job, she might understand how serious he really was about their cause and about her. And if he could bring her that far, then maybe it wasn't impossible to believe they'd end up in each other's arms.

Tristan was able to locate the entrance into the colony without using GPS and he warned Melanie to approach the first curve slowly. As expected, he saw his car was parked exactly where he'd left it, though now the roof was down.

"That man has a gun," Melanie said as they got closer. The car jerked to a stop. "Is he asleep?"

Tristan recognized Finch. "That's Finch. And don't worry. The gun's not loaded."

"What about her?" Melanie asked.

Tristan squinted against the morning sun and the dappled shade, then chuckled softly. Lily was curled up in the passenger seat of his Mercedes, also fast asleep. "Change of plan," he said. "You drive on into the camp and I'm going to take her and my car somewhere far away."

"Where are you going to go?" Melanie asked.

"I don't know," he said. "I'll figure that out when I get there."

"I should advise you that this looks like kidnapping to me."

"You're probably right. But I'm counting on convincing her that my motives are purely honorable."

Tristan got out of the car and quietly closed the door behind him. Finch was sitting in a nearby fold-up chair, snoring away. Tristan waved Melanie past him and she drove on, leaving him standing between the sleeping guard and his car. His footsteps crunched on the gravel as he made his way to the Mercedes.

He held his breath as he opened the driver's-side door and slipped behind the wheel. Once the key was in the ignition, Tristan started the car. To his surprise, the engine barely made a sound. Both the guard and Lily continued to sleep as he put the car into gear and slowly pulled away. He gathered speed as they approached the main road.

All he needed was a few minutes alone with her. If she'd just listen to him, he could make her understand.

LILY OPENED HER eyes to the bright glare of sunshine. It didn't surprise her that she'd fallen asleep. She'd spent the previous night with Tristan at the stone cottage, naked between brand-new sheets on an old iron bed.

Away from the camp, they'd found freedom in their solitude, and they'd been noisy and boisterous and bawdy with their pleasures, making love and drinking wine until dawn was just a few hours away.

The memory was so keen that Lily felt a shiver skitter through her body. Now, as she reexamined everything that had passed between them, she had to wonder what had been truth, and what had been a lie. Had everything between them been some kind of act? He'd obviously come to the colony with the hopes of getting the aunts to move off the land and away from everything they loved. But where did his charade begin and end?

He'd obviously decided to use her in his plan, to seduce her, hoping that she'd take his side simply to please him. It took a tremendous streak of arrogance to believe himself that powerful, and for Lily, it was one point she couldn't rationalize. Quinn didn't seem like an arrogant man. In the time they'd spent together, he'd shown himself to be just the opposite—humble and modest with a self-deprecating humor that she found wildly attractive.

Yawning, Lily stretched her arms over her head and turned in the seat, searching for a bit more leg room. But as she moved, she felt a strange sensation come over her, as if someone was watching her.

She sat up and glanced to her left, a tiny scream slipping from her lips as her gaze met his. "What? Where are we? What are you doing here?"

Lily scrambled out the passenger side door and backed away from the car. "Where are we?"

But she already knew the answer. They were parked outside the stone cottage.

Tristan smiled at her. "I'm not really sure. It's a nice view, don't you think?"

"I don't understand. How did you get me here?"

"You were sleeping. I just drove. You must have been really tired. You didn't move."

"You kidnapped me!"

"No. Technically, you were trespassing in my car and I decided drive away with you inside."

"No, no. Your car was parked on private property, so *you're* the one who was trespassing! I have every right to be in this car if it's on my property."

"Where did you get your law degree? Acme School of Law and Taxidermy? Plus, at no time has that property ever been considered yours."

The sharp edge of his words took her breath away

and sent a sudden flood of tears to her eyes. "There's a side of you we've never seen before. Wasn't that cruel." Lily shook her head and turned away, heading to the cottage.

Perhaps it was best to see the man in a true light, Lily mused. It would be so much easier to cast him from her life if he were flawed. Until today, she'd considered him a decent man. A man who could be trusted. Oh, how she'd been fooled.

She walked inside, letting the screen door slam behind her. Then she walked to the old fridge and pulled out a bottle of water, twisted off the cap and took a long slow drink. She heard the screen door slam again and then his footsteps.

Lily's shoulders slumped. "What do you want? Why did you bring me here?"

He set a paper bag down beside her as well as a steaming paper cup. "Coffee," he said. "And I bought you a cinnamon bun," He pulled a box out of the bag. "I thought we could have breakfast together and you could let me try to apologize for being a terrible jerk and a despicable liar."

Tristan arched his brow, glancing between her and the pastry. The enticing smell of yeast and cinnamon reached her nose and Lily's mouth began to water. The man sure knew how to set the stage for an apology, she mused. Cut flowers always made her sad and she'd never been a fan of chocolate candies. But give her freshly baked pastries or pie and she could be convinced to forgive even the most grievous of sins.

"What if I told you that I couldn't possibly forgive you?" she asked. "Would you take your buns and leave?"

"Probably not," he said. "I'd find some other excuse for staying, hoping that you'd change your mind and talk to me."

"How long were you going to go on with the charade?" she asked. "If Rose hadn't noticed your name on the stationery, how much longer were you going to keep up the lie?"

"I guess it never was a lie for me, Lily. When I saw what your aunts had built and how much you loved it, there was just no way I could work against you. So I quit my job and turned my attention to your case."

Lily's stomach growled and she pulled the box across the counter and opened it. Two cinnamon rolls from Main Street Bakery. He was almost as hard to resist as the pastry.

"Go ahead," he said. "You're hungry. You'll feel better once you've had something to eat."

She glanced over at him. "You really are the devil, aren't you?" Lily snatched a roll out of the box and took a huge bite, smearing frosting across her mouth. "This doesn't mean I forgive you. It simply means I'm hungry."

"Why were you sleeping in my car?" he asked.

She licked frosting off her fingers and met his gaze. "I had a few things I wanted to say to you before you left."

"I wasn't planning to leave, but I suppose this is a good time for you to say what you wanted to say. I'll listen."

Lily frowned. She'd had a whole speech planned, but now that she was sitting here, looking into his handsome face, she couldn't recall what she'd planned to say. "I'd rather hear your explanation first."

"It's simple, really," he began. "I came to the camp to make an offer to your aunts. It was a good plan until I met you. But from the minute I saw you, I needed to find a way to spend more time with you. I didn't care about my job, even though I tried to convince myself that being your friend was only a way to get closer to your aunts. But it had nothing to do with them. It was all about you."

Lily tried to detect some hint of dishonesty in his words. She already knew he was good at seducing women. But as she watched him attempt to explain his behavior, she realized that everything he said was coming directly from his heart.

"Why should I believe you?" she asked.

"Because I want to help you. And your aunts."

"But you work for the enemy."

He shook his head. "Not anymore. I quit. I realized the last thing I wanted to do was spend my professional life kicking three elderly women out of their homes. I can do better. That's why I went to law school in the first place. So I could help good people get a fair shake."

"You really quit your job?" Lily sighed softly. "What are you going to do?"

"I'm going to help you and your aunts keep the colony," he said. "You need a lawyer who can devote all his time to your case."

"But we can't pay you. Not what you were making with the law firm."

"I don't care. I have more than enough to tide me over until I find another job. Besides, when I told you about my past, I realized that after I joined the firm, I'd lost sight of why I'd become a lawyer in the first place. I made a promise to myself as a kid that I'd grow up to help people like me, people who have nowhere else to turn. People who can't afford to hire a big-city lawyer. I want to get to know my clients and be a part of their lives. So now I want to open up my own office and be in charge of my own schedule and clients."

Lily felt a rush of guilt overwhelm her. Over the past day, she'd thought the worst of Tristan Quinn and his motives. In her mind, he'd become the lowest form of enemy, the kind of man who would use a woman's affection for his own gain.

But there was no evidence that he'd done anything of the sort. She had to admit that his actions seemed to back up what he was saying. Perhaps she'd been right to trust him.

Until that moment, she hadn't realized what a toll this whole dispute had taken on her. The aunts were depending upon her to make sure everything came out the right way. And now that she realized Quinn was really on their side, she had hope that it would.

"It would probably be best for you to stay at camp," she said. "Everyone is still working hard to find some proof for our claim, but we're running out of possibilities. They're not going to be happy with you, so you'll probably need to face the inquisition and apologize. And then we'll have to hire another lawyer."

"You'll have me and Melanie. We worked with the firm. We know what they have. Trust me, Lily, we can get the job done."

She shook her head. "It's not up to me," she said.

He stared at her for a long moment, then took a step toward her. But Lily held her hand out. "I think it would be best if we left that part of our relationship in the past."

"You can't forgive me?"

"I'm not sure how I feel right now. And at the moment we have to concentrate on finding the proof we need to win."

He nodded, somewhat reluctantly. "All right. Why don't we go back to camp and let everyone know what happened."

Lily started for the door, then returned to pick up the cinnamon buns and the coffee. "You can drive," she said. "I'm going to eat breakfast."

THE "INQUISITION" WENT much better than Tristan could have anticipated. Everyone gathered in the dining hall and he stood in front them and confessed his deception. After that, he apologized and promised that he would do everything in his power to help save the colony if they agreed to keep him on as their attorney of record.

Lily had stayed for the first fifteen minutes but had wandered out as he'd begun to outline his professional qualifications and his education. He'd hoped that she might vouch for him, but it was clear that she intended to remain neutral in the verdict of whether he stayed or went.

That decision had required a long discussion, with his defenders and detractors being equally opinionated. But after his professional ethics were thoroughly questioned, Tristan was prepared to wrap things up— until the group decided to examine his personal life.

"I have a question," Aunt Violet said, raising her hand before standing. "It's been quite apparent from the start that you and my grand-niece have shared a special affection for each other. What are your plans where Lily is concerned?"

"I'm not sure what you mean," Tristan said.

"Are you in love with her?" Rose asked.

Tristan glanced around the room. His gaze met Melanie's and she quickly stood. "I'm not sure that question is within the scope of this inquiry. We should really stick to Mr. Quinn's professional qualifications."

"This inquiry can be whatever we want it to be," Rose said. "And I'd like an answer."

Tristan considered his options for a long moment, then decided that the truth would be best. "I don't have much experience with love," he said. "As a kid, my parents were more concerned with their own demons than showing my brothers and me what love was all about. We were on our own for a long time. I know I loved my brothers, even though we've never said it to each other out loud. Emotion like that was always considered a weakness."

It wasn't a complete answer, and as Tristan scanned the faces in the small crowd, he knew that they weren't sold on his explanation. "I care very much about Lily, about her happiness and the happiness of the people she loves—all of you. And when I think about my future, I imagine her in it." He shook his head. "Can I live without her? I probably would survive. Can I let her go? If I knew she'd be happier without me, I could. But I'm not sure I'd ever be able to forget her. If that's love, then yes, I love her."

He glanced over at the aunts and the three of them were dabbing their eyes with lacy handkerchiefs. His speech had obviously had some effect, just not on the right person. He should have said all those things to Lily. She needed to know how he felt.

But none of it would matter if he couldn't win the case for her and her aunts. He might be able to erase his deception from her memory, but he'd never be able to erase that failure.

Violet stood and moved to the front of the group. "I think we have the answers we need," she said. "Mr. Quinn, if you'll excuse us, we'll now discuss our options. Mr. Finch will inform you of our decision once we've made it."

"Thanks for your consideration," Tristan said. He walked out of the dining hall and into the cool night. The screen door slapped shut behind him and he drew a deep breath. The first stars were twinkling to life in the inky blue sky.

"Did you mean what you said in there?"

Her voice came out of the shadows and Tristan turned toward the sound. Lily sat in one of the old wicker chairs, her feet tucked up under her. "I thought you'd left," Tristan said.

"I just came out here to watch the sunset. There might not be many sunsets left from this vantage point."

"You should probably go back inside and let them know your vote. In or out."

"I've decided to recuse myself," Lily said. "I might be too biased to make a proper decision. I *have* slept with you. That could affect my opinion of you."

"And what is your opinion? I'd like to know."

"I'm still not sure," Lily said. "Everything seems to be in such a state of change. I don't want my feelings for you to be tied up in my fears."

He walked over and sat down on the chair next to hers. "What are you afraid of, Lily?"

"So many things I can't even start to tell you," she murmured.

He took her hand, slowly stroking the skin beneath her wrist. "Why don't you give me just one of your fears?"

"This is the only place I've ever been truly happy. The only place where I could be myself without any criticism. If I can't live here, where will I live?"

"If you have nowhere to go, you can stay with me," he said. "I'll always be around to help you, Lily. You can count on that."

A tiny smile curled the corners of her mouth. "Would you take the aunts in, too?"

"Sure, why not. We'll find a huge house. A big old Victorian. Or we'll find a piece of land and build three little cottages. Maybe we'll find a place that doesn't have such harsh winters. But I'm not going to worry too much, because I think everyone will be staying here."

She closed her eyes and took a deep breath. "That makes me feel better."

"How about another fear?" he said. "We can deal with two at once, can't we?"

"Okay… I'm afraid I won't be able to finish my paintings," she said.

"How many were you planning?"

"As many as I have inside me."

Tristan stood and pulled her to her feet. "That's something we can take care of right now." He tucked her hand into the crook of his arm. "Maybe you can get some sketches done tonight."

"You'd pose for me? Right now?"

"Sure. Do you want to go to your studio?"

She shook her head. "Meet me on the beach. I'll just go get my notebook and charcoal." She ran off in the direction of her cabin and Tristan watched as she disappeared into the dark.

He listened to the argument going on in the dining hall, then shook his head. As long as they were still speaking, they'd find a way through all the stress and troubles. Problems would be solved and decisions made. All he wanted in the end was a chance.

Tristan decided to sneak into the kitchen through the back door of the dining hall and search for a bottle of wine. He grabbed a half bottle of pinot noir from the counter. The argument had increased in ferocity and he winced, glad that he had been excused.

By the time he reached the beach, Lily was there, sitting in the dark, a blanket spread out over the sand. A small lantern sat on the sand next to her, providing enough light for her to draw by. He dropped down beside her and poured a glass of wine, taking a long sip.

"Where do you want me?" he asked.

"Nowhere," she said. "Not yet."

"What are we waiting for?" he asked.

"I'm waiting for that moon to move just beyond those trees so it will shine on the lake. Just fifteen minutes and it should be good."

"Are you going to make me go into the water?" he asked.

Lily nodded.

"And I have to take my clothes off?"

She nodded again.

"Am I missing something? Shouldn't there be some type of reward for my sacrifice? Standing stark naked, in a chilly lake. Exposing myself to pneumonia and other respiratory diseases."

Lily giggled and the sound was like music to his ears. He couldn't remember the last time he'd managed to make her laugh. Had it been a day? Or two? However many days, it had been too long. Her laughter was like oxygen to him. Without it, he couldn't seem to breathe.

He wanted to kiss her, but Tristan wasn't sure how she would react. If she refused, he'd be left to sort out her reasons for the rest of the night. Perhaps, if he waited, she'd kiss him and make her choice clear.

Tristan found himself longing for the time when they hadn't thought before they touched, when it had felt completely natural to tear at each other's clothes as they kissed. And then, that exquisite moment when their bodies became one.

Would they ever get back to that place? Or was this the beginning of the end for them? Tristan had never been in a relationship that hadn't burned out after a few weeks. But he'd always been happy for the end of it. This was different. This time he was desperate to make it last, just a day more, a week more.

He lay down on the blanket and stared up at the star-lit sky. A few seconds later, Lily curled up beside him, wrapping her arms around him. They didn't speak. Just lying next to each other was enough. The warmth from her body seeped into his as she moved closer.

He drifted off, surrendering to the exhaustion that the day had caused. When he opened his eyes again, the moon was high in the sky. "Lily?"

Tristan sat up and gave her a gentle shake. "Lily. It's time. The moon is out."

She rubbed her eyes, then sat up beside him. "The moon?"

Tristan got to his feet and reached for the hem of his T-shirt. He pulled it over his head, then tossed it aside. He reached for the button on his cargo shorts and Lily's eyes went wide.

She scrambled to her feet, struggling to gather her things at the same time. "I—I can't do this," she murmured. "I'm sorry. I have to go."

Tristan stood on the beach, watching her once again disappear into the dark. He didn't follow her. There was nothing he could say to her that would make her feel differently about him. Whatever they'd shared in the past was over, and the sooner he came to accept that, the better.

Cursing softly, he stepped out of his shorts and boxer briefs, then walked naked across the sand. The water was chilly at first, stealing his breath with each inch that touched his skin. Finally, he dove in, the temperature shocking his body and clearing his mind.

He'd get over her. He just had to push every single thought of her out of his mind.

8

LILY OPENED HER eyes to the sounds of shouting and the dining hall bell ringing. She brushed her hair out of her eyes and sat up, pulling the quilts up around her to ward off the chill in her cabin.

A few seconds later, she heard footsteps on her porch, followed by a knock at the door. "Lily? Lily, are you awake?"

Lily recognized the voice of Evaleen Deschanter, a folksinger who'd been coming to the colony for the last ten years.

"Come in," she called.

Evaleen stumbled inside, gasping for breath, her color high. She pressed her hand to her chest. "You— you have to come. It's Daisy. She fainted and hit her head. They called the ambulance and the paramedics will be here in a few minutes. Tristan said he'd take you to the hospital."

Overwhelming fear seemed to crush her body and for a long moment, Lily couldn't make herself move or speak—or even breathe. Her aunts had been relatively healthy over the years. There had never been cause to call an ambulance. But Lily knew that such good health for three seventy-year-old women wouldn't last long.

"Is she conscious now?" Lily asked.

"Semi-conscious," Evaleen said. "I think she's trying to say something but the words aren't coming out right."

Lily's mind immediately went to a stroke and she knew it was essential to get Daisy to the hospital as soon as possible. "I'll be right there."

As she scrambled to find something to wear, Lily heard the siren approach. She finally found a pair of shoes and left the cabin in a cotton blouse, capris and a pair of sandals. She grabbed a sweater on her way, then returned for her wallet. She might need ID for something.

By the time she got down to the dining hall, the paramedics had already loaded Daisy into the ambulance. Violet and Rose were standing together outside the car, both of them on the verge of tears. Lily ran over to them and gave them each a hug.

"She's going to be fine," Lily assured them. "I think it's best if you stay here and Tristan and I go with her to the hospital. Once things are stable and she can have visitors, we'll come back and get you two."

"No, we want to go with her. Now."

"Both of you need to relax or you'll end up in an ambulance yourselves. Waiting around the hospital for hours is going to be exhausting. Trust me, as soon as I know anything, I'll call."

The paramedics closed the rear door of the ambulance and Lily told them she'd meet them at the hospital. She quickly gave her aunts a hug, then hurried over to Tristan's car. He helped her inside and closed the door behind her.

Determined to stay strong, Lily fought the rush of emotion that threatened to pull her under. But the moment Tristan slipped behind the wheel, the first tears started to trickle down her cheeks.

"Hey," he said, wrapping his arm around her shoulders. "It's going to be all right." He pulled her close and kissed the top of her head. "We're going to make sure she has the best doctors."

"I'm not sure I can handle this," Lily said, sobbing. "I know I have to be brave, but the reality is too much to bear. Someday, I'm going to be all alone. And my life with the aunts will be just a memory. Just the idea of that frightens me."

Tristan pulled out onto the main road, keeping his eyes on the ambulance in the distance. They were heading to the hospital in Buffalo, the closest hospital to the colony. The ten-minute trip seemed to take twice that much time. Lily focused on her breathing, in and out, in and out, counting each one.

"We're here," Tristan said. He quickly pulled into a parking spot and grabbed Lily's hand as they hurried through the doors of the emergency room. When they got to the desk, Tristan explained who they were. The nurse showed them to a waiting area.

"Would it be all right if Lily went in to be with her

aunt?" Tristan asked the nurse. "I think Daisy would do better if Lily was there with her."

"I'm sorry, you'll have to wait here."

They sat down together and Lily held tight to his arm. "Thank you. For speaking. I'm not sure I could have gotten out a word without bursting into tears."

Tristan smiled. "It's all right." He wrapped his arm around her shoulders and pulled her close, gently rubbing her back. Lily wasn't sure how she'd be handling this on her own, but she felt so much better because Tristan was with her.

"Excuse me, are you here with Daisy Pigglestone?"

Lily looked up at the nurse. "I—I am. We are. Is she all right?"

"I need to get some information from you. Would you be able to provide that?"

Lily nodded, then stood.

"Can you come with me?" the nurse said.

Tristan and Lily followed the woman into a small office. She gave Lily a small stack of forms that Lily carefully filled out, answering questions as best as she could for Daisy. They'd never been through anything like this.

"Do you have medical power of attorney for your aunt, Miss Harrison?"

"I—I don't understand. What is that?"

"Did you ever sign papers that a lawyer prepared giving you the power to make decisions for your aunts?"

"They make their own decisions," Lily said.

"No," Tristan said to the nurse. "She doesn't have medical power of attorney."

"Is there anyone who can make decisions for her?" the woman asked. "A husband? Children, perhaps?"

"Does she need someone to do that?" Lily asked. "Can't she make her own decisions? I want to see her."

"She has two sisters," Tristan said to the nurse. "We'll call them if decisions need to be made. I'll make sure we have some arrangements made about power of attorney before the end of the day. Can Lily go back and see Daisy?"

"Let me find out where they are with her," the nurse said.

She gathered up the papers and left the room. Lily drew a deep breath. "I didn't know things would be so complicated. I feel like I've been living life in this fairy-tale world but disaster has been just outside the front door all along. I should have known about these things. Power of attorney. Why didn't I know about that?"

"Because your aunts have always been healthy and able to handle their own affairs. I think it would be best if all three of them gave you medical power of attorney."

"I don't want that. That means I'll have to be the one to pull the plug if there is ever a need. I can't make decisions like that."

Lily pushed out of her chair and ran out into the lobby. She felt as if the walls were closing in on her. How could she have been so blind? This was the real world, where people got sick and died. Where tragedy happened and life was difficult. And no one had ever prepared her to handle the darker part of life.

She walked outside and sat down on a low bench, drawing in a deep breath and letting it out slowly. Life could turn on a dime. Didn't that mean a person had to grab happiness where they found it? And though she admired her aunts for facing the world as independent women, Lily was beginning to realize that it wasn't the life she wanted. She didn't want to be strong every moment of every day. She didn't want to fall asleep all alone and wake up the same way.

She drew her knees up and pressed her forehead against them, pulling herself into a tight little ball. She'd always made her own choices, but now she needed to put aside her fears and insecurities and help her aunts make it through this crisis.

"Lily?"

She glanced over to see Tristan standing in the doorway. "The doctor wants to see you. Daisy is all right. She's resting comfortably."

A weak "oh" was all she could manage before the tears started again. But she took another breath and brushed the tears away. "Thank you," she said, her jaw tight.

Lily marched back into the lobby of the emergency room. A young man, barely older than she was, approached her and held out his hand.

"I'm Dr. Jacobsen."

"Lily Harrison," she said. "How is my aunt?"

"She's stable and resting. She's had a small stroke. We've given her some medication that can prevent further strokes, but we'd like to move her to a larger hospital with a critical care unit that can provide a full range of testing. We can call for an air ambulance or have her driven there in a regular ambulance. The drive would take just over an hour."

"Flying might be too stressful for her. I don't think she's been in a plane in fifteen years."

"Then we'll send her in a regular ambulance. If you'd like, you can ride along with her."

Lily threw her arms around the doctor's neck and gave him a fierce hug. "Thank you. Thank you so much."

He patted her on the shoulder. "Why don't you come back and see your aunt? She's having some trouble speaking, but that will improve with time. Stay calm and just speak to her in a soothing voice."

Lily nodded. "When will we leave for the other hospital?"

"It will take us a couple of hours to make the arrangements. If you'd like to run home and pack a bag, you can go in for a quick visit now. If not, just let the nurse know when you're ready."

Lily nodded, then turned to Tristan. "I'm going to ride in the ambulance with Daisy. Can you go back to the camp and help make arrangements to take Violet and Rose to the hospital? I'll find them a hotel nearby. I'll stay with them."

"You can stay with me," Tristan said. "I have a nice place on the river."

"Maybe…it'll depend on how things go. Pack a bag

for me? I give you permission to go through my underwear drawer."

"You actually have an underwear drawer?" he asked. "Is there anything in it?"

She couldn't help but laugh and the act seemed to shatter the tension between them. "Could you also take care of preparing the powers of attorney for my aunts? We should all have the same authority."

"I'll take care of it," Tristan said.

"All right, then," she said. Lily pushed up on her toes and gave him a soft, lingering kiss. "I love you," she murmured.

She saw the expression on his face when she said the words, but she wasn't sure what it meant. Was it shock? Discomfort? Or confusion? Lily wasn't going to wait around and find out. "See you soon," she said before she turned and walked away.

As she entered the lobby, she smiled to herself. She really didn't care how he reacted. She'd expressed her true feelings at that very moment and she wasn't ashamed. She didn't wish she could take the words back. After all he'd done for her this day, Lily knew it was true. Tristan Quinn was a man she could love. Now he just had to decide whether he could love her.

TRISTAN UNLOCKED THE door to his condo, then stepped inside. He'd been back and forth all day between the hospital and his place. Lily had decided to come home with him, and he'd wanted to do something to surprise her.

"What's going on here?" she asked as she walked inside.

The lights were off, but he'd lit thirty or forty candles and placed them around the spacious living and dining room. The golden light flickered off the pale gray walls and white woodwork, giving the usually tranquil interior a romantic edge.

"I was suddenly thinking I'd enjoy this place a lot more if it didn't have electricity, like my cabin at the colony. I thought I'd try it out for an evening."

She smiled. "This isn't an attempt at romance?"

"Why would I try to get romantic with you?"

Lily turned and faced him. "Because I told you that I loved you."

"Oh, that," he said, nodding. Tristan held out his hand. "Come with me. I'll show you what I did because of that."

Lily set her bags down on the floor and put her hand in his. Tristan led her through the living room and then down the bedroom hallway. They walked through his candlelit bedroom to the bathroom.

"I don't have a lake," he said. "But I do have a very deep and roomy whirlpool tub all set for a little swim."

Lily sat down on the edge of the tub. "Rose petals?"

"I saw it on the internet," Tristan admitted. "But I thought of the champagne and strawberries all by myself." He laid his phone on the vanity and pressed play. A soft jazz standard filled the room.

Tristan returned to the tub and started filling it with warm water. He poured in some bubble bath. Before long, bubbles floated on the surface of the water.

Then he turned to Lily. "This is because you said you loved me."

"I wasn't sure I should have said it," Lily murmured as she began to undress.

"I'm glad you did," Tristan murmured, stepping behind her to take the clothes she discarded.

Tristan had marveled at Lily's exquisite body in many different settings—outside, in the still of the lake; beneath a cloud of mosquito netting; and then in the quiet interior of the stone cottage, wrapped in a rough wool blanket, her hair damp from the rain.

He'd brought her to her peak in a sun-splashed bit of forest and on the chaise in her studio. But he had to admit that Lily naked in his very own bathroom was the best of all encounters so far.

"What's going through that head of yours?" Tristan asked, holding out his hand to help her into the tub.

"I'm a little nervous," Lily replied, slowly sinking down into the water. "Is this gratitude? Or is it seduction?" She sat in the center of the large whirlpool, completely naked, her legs pulled up in front of her, her hands clasped around her shins. He hadn't realized how tanned her body was until it was contrasted against the pure white bubbles.

He handed her a glass of champagne, then fed her a strawberry. She smiled as she quickly drank the champagne. Lily held out the flute to be refilled.

"Easy there. It's going to go to your head if you drink that fast."

"Isn't that the point? Are you just going to sit there waiting on me, or are you going to join me?"

"If I get into that tub, you're going to be in all sorts of trouble," he said.

"I might drown if I'm left in here alone for too long," Lily teased.

"I promise to pull you out before that happens."

Lily handed him the champagne flute and sank down into the bubbling water. "This really is luxury. A girl could get used to this."

"Is there anything else I can get you?"

She picked up her foot and hung it over the edge of the tub. "You could massage my feet," she said. Lily turned and braced her back on the side of the tub and hung both feet over the edge.

Tristan sat opposite her, then stripped off his T-shirt and crossed his legs in front of him. He took one delicate foot in his grasp and slowly began to massage it, working his fingers from her heel to her toes and lingering on the arch.

"Daisy looked much better today," Tristan said. "Even between my morning and afternoon visit, I could see the improvement."

"Her speech is almost back to normal. Thank God it wasn't a major stroke. The doctor thinks she should be able to go home in a few days, but she might need physical therapy." Lily paused. "I don't know how I would have handled this if you hadn't been here to help."

Tristan gave her foot a squeeze, then pressed a kiss to the bottom of it.

"Why do we have to make this all so complicated?" Lily asked. She pulled her feet back into the tub, then rested her arms on the edge, staring directly into his eyes. "I can crawl into your bed and we can see what happens and it doesn't have to change anything between us."

Tristan reached out and toyed with a curl that grazed her cheek. "Shouldn't we know what we want?"

"No!" Lily cried. "And we don't have to. We shouldn't have to plan our entire lives just because we fell madly in love for a few months."

Tristan forced a smile. Now he understood. For Lily, love was something finite, a state of happiness that had a beginning and an end. Could he play by her rules? Could he accept that his love for her would last a lifetime while hers might fade quickly?

He wasn't sure he'd ever be able to predict her thoughts. Lily Harrison seemed to be wired differently from the women he'd known. But he was beginning to understand why she'd chosen to reject the greed and artifice of some members of her family and cast her lot with a trio of free-spirited septuagenarians.

"Are you sure you don't want to join me?" she asked.

This was not going at all as Tristan had imagined it, but he didn't care. Resisting Lily was had never been his strong suit.

She slowly stood, the scented water sluicing over her gleaming skin. He grabbed her waist and picked her up, lifting her over the edge of the tub. When they reached the bed, Tristan pulled her down next to him, then leaned over and dropped a kiss on her lips.

Lily sighed, her hand drifting down to his belly. She wrapped her fingers around his hard shaft and

Tristan drew in a sharp breath. Her touch had such an incredible power over his body.

Every nerve from his fingers to his toes came alive, crackling with anticipation, waiting for the next sensory experience to race to his brain. The silken feel of her hair between his fingers. The scent of her skin, a mix of sunshine and lavender soap. The taste of her mouth, tonight a mixture of champagne, strawberries and a hint of the cinnamon roll she'd devoured earlier. She was beautiful in so many ways that she pushed all rational thought from his head.

Tristan slipped his hand around her nape and pulled her into a long, lazy kiss. It seemed as if the world had finally slowed down enough for them to enjoy each other. Until this point, there had always been reasons not to completely surrender. But the lies and ulterior motives had been swept away now, leaving them this moment.

He wanted it to be perfect in a way he never had before. This might be the last time. Before, it had mostly been about their physical satisfaction, and Tristan had taken care to be a generous lover. But tonight he wanted her to see him as more than just a guy who was very good at seduction. There was more at stake tonight with Lily, yet he wasn't sure exactly what. He just sensed that what happened between them here, in this room, would set the course for their future. "So no promises, no plans."

"You only need to make me one promise," she murmured.

"Anything."

"Promise me that you'll do everything you can to help my aunts."

Tristan knew there was a good chance that when they took their fight to court, they'd lose. And that his promise wouldn't make a difference. But the look on her beautiful face was so vulnerable, so filled with worry, that he nodded.

Tonight, he wanted to be the guy who could make all her wishes come true. He stood up and slowly removed his clothes.

Lily watched him, her lips curled into a playful smile, her eyes sparkling with anticipation.

He leaned over and gave her a sweet, tempting kiss, running his tongue along the crease of her lips. Then he started to kiss his way down her body, from her jaw to her throat to her breasts.

Her skin was still slick as he captured a nipple between his lips, sucking at it until it was hard and swollen. When Tristan moved to her other breast, Lily moaned, pulling him into another kiss before he continued.

She smelled like the scent of the bubble bath, a mix of citrus that he found intoxicating. His mouth moved lower, pressing a line of kisses to her belly. When he gently pressed her thighs to the bed, she whispered his name, her fingers tangling in his hair, pulling him toward her.

He knew exactly what she liked and brought her to the edge quickly. But this time, Tristan didn't want to tease her. Instead, he pulled a condom from the bedside table and quickly sheathed himself.

"Hurry," she murmured, reaching out for him.

When he was ready, she guided him inside her. He barely moved before Lily dissolved into an orgasm and he understood her plea for haste. She spasmed around him as he drove into her in long, smooth strokes that stole the last bit of release from her body.

Tristan slowed his pace, waiting for her to recover, wanting to bring her back to the edge yet again. He pressed a kiss to her shoulder, then pulled her arms above her head, clasping her wrists with one hand.

"Would you like to try that again?" he whispered.

"Yes, please," she replied. "Again and again."

"TOMORROW, I HAVE TO depose Miss Luella Helmsworth," Tristan said to her as they luxuriated in another bubble bath—this time together.

"That's tomorrow?" Lily asked.

Tristan nodded. "She's going to explain, under oath, that Edward Pigglestone arranged for a deed that would gave your aunts ownership of the lake and the surrounding land and all the buildings. She is the only proof we have regarding your great-great-grandfather's intent."

"Is it enough?" Lily asked.

"This is what I wanted to talk to you about," Tristan said. "When I originally came out to the camp, I had an offer that I was supposed to present."

"But you didn't."

"Because I wasn't sure the aunts would have considered it. But after what happened with Daisy, they may want to now." Tristan reached into the bubbly water and grabbed a loofah scrub. He moved to the end of the tub. "Lean forward," he said.

"I can't believe they'd accept any offer, no matter what the circumstances. We have to continue the fight."

Tristan slowly began to scrub her back. "I understand you don't want to admit defeat before the case is even before the court."

"What was the offer?"

"Are you sure you want to hear it?"

Lily nodded, the damp tendrils of her hair falling around her face. "I should hear it. I can't be stubborn about this."

"Here's the thing," he began. "If you turn down any attempts to settle now and then you lose the case, you and the aunts will end up with nothing. No money to purchase a new place you can all call home. No homes to live in—they go with the property. No place for all your friends to gather."

"They would be crushed," Lily said.

"If Miss Helmsworth gives us a hook to hang our case on, then I think we'll be all right. But beyond that, we've found no documentation that says the aunts' father ever intended to give them the lake and land to keep."

"Maybe you're right that what happened with Daisy may change their minds," Lily said. "What if she can't go back to her house? What if she has to stay in the hospital for a long stretch? Or what if one of the other aunts gets sick and they have to go to the hospital? They're not going to want to be separated."

"The offer was three million a piece. That's more

than enough to buy them another property wherever they want to go. They don't use a tenth of the property they're on now."

"That's lot of money," she said.

"It is. I can call the firm and find out if that offer still stands. If it does, then we can take it to the aunts this morning."

"Don't we have some time to think about this?" Lily said.

"If we depose Luella and she doesn't have any relevant information, then there's no reason for the firm to offer a settlement. They'll push ahead with the case and the aunts could get nothing."

"We need to go to the hospital and tell them," she said. "They've been so stubborn before, but maybe they'll change their minds."

"There's nothing in this for you, Lily," he said.

"I didn't expect there would be,' she said. "I'm fine. I have plenty to get by."

Tristan's deposition started at 1 p.m. and it was nearly 10 a.m. by the time they parked in the hospital lot. Tristan dialed Forster and Dunlap and asked for Reggie Dunlap. Lily listened on the car's speaker.

"Reggie, it's Tristan Quinn. I'm about to meet with the Pigglestone sisters and I was wondering if the most recent offer you made to them is still good."

"Are the old ladies softening a bit?" Reggie asked.

"We'd just like to consider all our options, Reggie."

"I hear one of them is in the hospital. Nothing serious, I hope."

"No, nothing that a few days rest won't cure," Tristan replied, glancing over at Lily.

"Yeah, the offer is still good. But only until noon."

Tristan cursed beneath his breath. "All right. I'll get back to you."

"Is that bad?" Lily asked.

"Yeah. It's means that Reggie has his own doubts about Luella. He's telling us to take it or leave it. The clock is ticking."

They got out of the car and hurried into the hospital. After a stop in Daisy's room, they found the three sisters in the solarium, playing cards at a small table. Daisy was holding her own cards, though at a rather clumsy angle. Another sign of progress, Lily mused.

"Oh, look who's come for a visit!" Violet cried. "Tristan is here."

Lily smiled as she watched him circle the table, kissing each of them on the hand in greeting. When he'd finished, he grabbed a pair of chairs from a nearby table and held one out for Lily.

"Would you like to join the game?" Violet asked. "We're playing Hearts. Lily knows how to play, don't you, dear?"

"Actually, we came here to talk to you about something very important." Lily nodded to Tristan and he carefully explained the latest offer and his concerns about Luella.

The aunts listened patiently, asking questions every now and then and nodding when Tristan offered his opinion. He wrapped up his explanation, then asked them what they wanted to do.

"Well, I certainly don't need another three million dollars. I have plenty of money," Rose said.

"So do I. I'd rather have our little camp on Fence Lake," said Violet.

"You don't understand," Lily said. "You could lose the camp. At least with the money, you could build something new."

"You could disassemble what you have at the camp and move the whole thing to another location," suggested Tristan.

"But our location is perfect. Why would we want to leave?"

"You're taking a huge risk," Tristan said. "This is all or nothing."

She reached out and placed her hand on his shoulder. She could hear the frustration growing in his voice and Lily sensed he was about to lose his temper. "I think they do understand," Lily said softly. "And they have considered the consequences. We should let the ladies get back to their game."

"I have a bad feeling about this," he muttered. "Why did you give up so easily?" he asked as they made their way out of the hospital.

"Once they've made up their collective mind, nothing is going to change it."

"It's a huge, huge risk," he said.

"I'm sure they understand that," she said. Lily pushed up on her toes and gave him a quick kiss. "You better get going. You don't want to keep Miss Luella waiting."

He nodded. "I'll come and pick you up in a couple of hours. We'll go out and get some dinner."

"Good luck," Lily said. "I'll cross my fingers for you."

"If you have any other superstitious behavior you'd like to try, go right ahead. We'll need everything we can get."

He kissed her again, this time pulling her into his arms and bending her back. Lily glanced around and noticed a number of patients and staff watching them. "Maybe we should have another bath when we get home," she murmured.

"I'll look forward to it."

THE ATMOSPHERE INSIDE the conference room was tense. Depositions in civil cases were usually fairly straightforward. But the deposition of Miss Luella Helmsworth, former secretary to Edward Pigglestone, wasn't made easier by the fact that Luella enjoyed being the center of attention.

Bernie had found her living in a pleasant retirement home in California. They'd sent a limousine to pick her up from the airport and put her up in a nice downtown hotel, which had only added to her excitement.

After a pleasant lunch, Tristan brought Luella down to a small conference room. A court reporter awaited them and he settled Luella in a comfortable chair and took his place across the table from her. A few minutes later, Reggie arrived and Tristan made the introductions.

"Is he the bad guy?" Luella asked. "Must I answer the questions he asks? I can be a hostile witness. I used to watch *Law & Order*. I know exactly how to do it."

Reggie shot Tristan a glare and Tristan shrugged. "Ms. Helmsworth, please answer every question posed to you with the absolute truth," Tristan said.

This was not a good way to start. He'd have to find a way to keep Luella focused.

"All right, but did you call me *Ms.* Helmsworth? I believe in women's rights and I respect feminists, but I have never understood the use of Ms. instead of Miss. Ms. It sounds like miserable, which I suppose most spinsters are. Unless you have a satisfying career. Which I did."

"Let's talk about that career," Tristan said, trying to get her back on track. "Do you remember when Edward Pigglestone built the three houses for his daughters on Fence Lake?"

"I do," she said. "In fact, I designed them."

Tristan's eyebrow shot up. "You designed them?"

"Yes. He used to call those girls his three little Piggles. So I drew out a house made of stone, a house made of wood and a house made of straw. It was like a fairy tale come true. He wanted them close by and it was a clever plan. He gave them the money for the dining hall and the little theater, too."

"You remember this?"

"Oh, yes. All the construction bills crossed my desk. I'd double-check them and then show them to Edward. He'd approve and I'd have bookkeeping write the checks."

"The three women have been paying the property taxes for years now. Do you know how that came about?"

"He instructed me to have them start paying the taxes right after the houses were built. He thought, since they would eventually hold the deed to the property, that they should get accustomed to paying the taxes."

"So Edward had every intention of giving the girls the deed to the property?"

"Yes, he did. I distinctly remember the paperwork being delivered to the office. It was going to be a Christmas gift. They were all coming home for the holidays."

"The girls claimed that they never received a deed. There was no transfer recorded with the county. Is it your testimony that Edward Pigglestone made arrangements to deed the property to his three daughters?"

"Of course. There wasn't much use for that land. Too far from town, too many mosquitoes and no sewer line."

Tristan couldn't believe the wealth of info about Edward Pigglestone that Luella had tucked away in her mind. But as he continued to question her, he could see she was starting to tire.

"You know what I could use?" she asked, leaning closer to Tristan.

"A break?"

"No! A drink! I had this lovely drink last night at the hotel. A peach bellini. Could you whip one of those up for me? It's five o'clock somewhere!"

"Maybe we should wrap this up," Reggie said.

"But we just got here," Luella said.

"I'd like to study what we learned today and get together tomorrow morning," Reggie said. "Perhaps Mr. Quinn could take you out for that…"

"Bellini," she said. "Peach bellini."

Reggie stood up and motioned Tristan over. "You've got your prize witness, Quinn. She'll say almost anything you want her to say."

"I did not coach her. All those answers were spontaneous."

"And borderline wacky," Reggie said. "We're not going to be a part of this. I don't have any questions for this witness."

He started for the door. "Oh, by the way, did they take the deal?"

"No," Tristan said.

"Pity. I don't like the idea of tossing three old women out into the snow. But I will enjoy beating your ass."

"That was rather rude," Luella said after Reggie had gone.

"We don't get along very well."

"You seem to be a very nice young man. Are we going to get that drink now?"

Tristan gathered his things. "Yes, we will. We can chat a bit more about Edward and his three little Piggles."

9

THE TRIAL LASTED just two days. Both parties had agreed to forgo a jury and asked for a judge's verdict instead. Tristan had had only four weeks to gather evidence and prepare the defendants' case.

The plaintiffs had had over a year, but the trial date had been set a while ago and the sisters had ignored the notice—until he'd entered the picture.

Lily and the three Pigglestone sisters sat in the gallery of the courtroom. They'd gotten the call that morning that the judge was ready to announce his decision in the *Pigglestone Family Foundation versus Violet, Daisy and Rose Pigglestone* case.

Tristan had presented a well-organized argument that revolved around squatter's rights. The sisters had lived on the property for years without interference, had paid property taxes and made improvements by building the guest cabins. The judge appeared receptive, but the law was on the plaintiffs' side.

The property had been listed in Edward's will and

had been specifically left to the family foundation. Luella's testimony had been entered into the record, but even if Edward had had plans to deed the property to his three daughters, there was no record that he had done so. The odds weren't in their favor.

The judge walked in and took a seat behind the bench. "I've come to a decision. With such a large property at stake and family ties at risk, this was a very difficult case to adjudicate. Unfortunately, the evidence weighs ever so slightly on the side of the plaintiffs, and I rule in their favor."

Tristan felt the air leave the room and for a long moment, no one made a noise. He had known the odds, but he was still hoping that good would win out. Nice people didn't always finish first, but just this once, he'd hoped that the Pigglestone sisters would.

"Your honor, with all due respect, we're going to appeal."

"Mr. Quinn, I'm going to delay any transfer of property for one year. If you can find additional proof of your claim, you can relitigate. If not, this time will give your clients a chance to make future plans."

Reggie Dunlap stood up. "Your honor, this matter has already dragged out for three years. This has become a financial burden for my clients and—"

"Mr. Dunlap, I've read the financials of the Pigglestone Family Foundation. They have plenty of money to get them through the next ten or fifteen years, let alone the next twelve months. I will see you all in one year. At that time, we will close this matter and move on."

"Thank you, your honor."

Tristan turned to face Lily and her aunts. They all had various expressions of shock and sadness on their faces. He bent close, bracing his hands on the wood rail in front of them. "Listen, it isn't over. You have another summer at the colony and we have a whole year to find more evidence to support our claim. We came very close. It isn't going to take much to push this decision back to our side."

Lily nodded. "Tristan is right. We have another year. We just have to keep a positive attitude. All of us know that we're on the right side. And we'll find something that will help prove that."

"Yes," Violet said. She reached to grab her sisters' hands. "We know what Daddy wanted for us. Tristan will find a way to prove our case." She stood, tipping her chin up defiantly. "Now, we'd better be on our way. Everyone at camp is planning a surprise party for us to celebrate our victory. Let's all try to be happy."

Tristan packed up his papers and slipped them inside his briefcase. Lily appeared at his side and wrapped her arms around his waist, giving him a gentle hug.

"I'm sorry," he said in a tight voice.

"You did your best," she said. "I know that. And we will appeal. Besides, who can say what we might find in the next year? I can devote a lot more time to discovery now that the season is winding down." She paused. "Tristan, I talked to the aunts and they want to pay you for all the work you did. We can afford it."

"No, it's all right. It will be my first pro bono case as a sole practitioner. This was the way it was meant to be. I always wanted to have my own practice, maybe in a smaller town."

"Don't you want to work in the city?" Lily asked.

"I'm not sure the city's for me anymore. I enjoyed my six weeks at the colony. Fresh air, spending my days in shorts and a T-shirt, staying up late, sleeping in on rainy days. Life is too short, Lily, and it's time I started enjoying myself a little more."

They walked out of the courthouse and into the late afternoon sun. "I was actually thinking that I've been enjoying myself too much," she said. "I've been living at the colony because it was safe and easy. I dabbled at my art and occasionally produced a piece I was proud of. But I was stuck. I wasn't growing as a woman or as an artist."

"So I'm moving to the country and you're moving to the city?"

"Not exactly," she said. "I might go to Portugal."

Tristan tried to hide his surprise. He'd just assumed they'd continue to see each other over the winter. There was no reason why she couldn't paint somewhere in Minnesota.

"You could come with me," she said.

"I could," he said. "But I have to figure out how I'm going to make a living. I've got a mortgage and a car payment, both of which are going to be more than I can afford."

"I have money," she said. "You wouldn't need to worry."

There it was, Tristan thought to himself. They'd

managed to avoid the issue of her money until now. "So, you're offering to make me a kept man?"

Lily shook her head as she waited for him to open the car door. "I've always wondered how you'd react to the offer," she said. "In my experience, there are two types of guys. Those who can hardly wait to spend someone else's money and those who could never wrap their heads around the idea of a woman controlling the purse strings."

She slipped inside the car and Tristan shut the door, then circled around to the driver's side of the Mercedes. He tossed his briefcase in the backseat, then got behind the wheel. "I won't lie, it would be difficult for me, Lily. I've scratched my way through life, always hanging off the bottom rung of the ladder. I've been homeless, I've eaten meals out of garbage dumpsters, I've stolen food from convenience stores when I was so hungry I couldn't sleep at night."

"It's just money," Lily said. "I didn't do anything to make it. I just happened to be born into a particular family. And it does make life easier. But I'm not going to apologize for that. I use what I need and I leave the rest."

"I'm not faulting you. You are the kindest person I've ever known. There isn't an ounce of greed or selfishness in you. But I'm a proud man. And you've made it clear that you believe that our relationship has an end date. If you don't want a life with me, I have to make my own way."

"You haven't exactly been Mr. Emotional with me,

either." Lily sighed. "I don't want to talk about this anymore. It's…unseemly."

Tristan ran his hands along the steering wheel, laughing to himself. "Unseemly." He paused. "So, to get back to the subject. No, I will not be coming to Portugal with you. What are you planning to do in Portugal?"

"Paint," she said.

"Good," he said.

He put the car into gear and pulled out of the courthouse parking lot. They'd never argued like that before, Tristan mused. Any disagreements had been smoothed over with a kiss or a simple apology. But this conflict ran so much deeper.

They were fundamentally different, and had been from the very moment they were born. He'd never felt so far away from her as he did now. Tristan reached out and gently took her hand, then brought it to his lips.

"Let's just forget that conversation," he said.

"I think that would be best," Lily said.

She drew away from him, turning her face toward the window. He couldn't tell if she was angry or upset, but when she drew in a ragged breath, he knew she was crying.

They rode the rest of the way to the colony in silence. Tristan wanted to explain, but he knew that it would never come out right.

When he pulled up in front of the dining hall, he saw the lights strung from the rafters. Dance music from the 1940s drifted out on the evening air. The party was already in full swing. The sisters, chauffeured by

Finch, had arrived a few minutes before Tristan and Lily, and had broken the news of the judge's ruling.

"I don't feel much like dancing," Lily murmured.

"Or celebrating," he added. "I think I'm going to drive back to the city tonight. I've got a lot of loose ends I need to take care of. I've got to start making a living."

"I'm sure your own practice will make you happy."

Tristan wanted to tell her that she was the only thing in the world that had made him truly happy. But he didn't want to sound like some foolish sap. They'd spent a wonderful two months together and now it was time to get on with the rest of his life.

"Can I walk you up to your cabin?" he asked.

Lily shook her head. "That would be asking for trouble," she said.

"Why is that?"

"You know how it would go. You'd kiss me goodnight. I'd kiss you back. All the anger we're feeling right now would turn to desperation. Oops, there go all our clothes and we'd be in bed together."

He chuckled softly. "You're probably right. We never have been good at controlling our impulses."

"It's what I loved most about us," Lily said, joining in the joke. She shifted to face him. "I guess I'll just say 'see you soon,' then."

He nodded. "See ya, Lily. Take care. And call me if you need anything or if something comes up with the lawsuit."

"I will."

"The aunts, too. Anything they need. Just call."

She opened the car door and stepped out. Tristan pressed his hand to his chest. It felt like she was tearing his heart out, the pain taking his breath away.

And then the door slammed shut behind her and Tristan had no choice but to leave. He watched her walk over to the dining hall and he waited for her to look back, just once. But she pulled the screen door open and stepped inside.

"Goodbye, Lily," he murmured.

Ending it wasn't easy. And he wasn't even sure it was what he wanted. But it had lasted much longer than he ever thought it would. And it had all been better than he could have ever imagined it might be.

She'd found a place in his life, however short-term it might have been, but he'd always remember how it had felt to lose his heart to Lily Harrison. Maybe someday, he'd be able to retrieve all the pieces she'd kept. But until then, he'd have to live with what was left.

THE SNOW HAD been falling since midmorning and the streets in downtown Minneapolis were getting more treacherous with every hour that passed.

Lily gripped the steering wheel of her Mini Cooper, peering out into the weather as she crept along. She'd been legally driving since Thanksgiving and was now the proud owner of a Minnesota driver's license. Most of her miles had been spent on the snow-covered roads around the lake and her stone cottage.

But today she'd had to come into the city and she'd been confident enough to venture into traffic during clear weather. This snowstorm had caught her by surprise. She scanned the street for an empty parking spot and when she saw one, deftly steered the Mini into the spot.

Lily drew a deep breath and sighed. She'd had every intention of spending the winter in Portugal, but she'd found herself caught up in a creative whirlwind that she'd been hesitant to interrupt.

She'd been painting and sculpting and at the same time renovating the stone cottage and turning it into a home. But of all the things she'd tackled, the driving had been the most difficult.

Lily got out of the car, then opened the hatchback and withdrew a plastic-wrapped canvas. Then she locked the car and fed the meter before hurrying down the street to the Welbrun Gallery.

She pushed open the wide glass doors and walked inside, pausing on the rug to brush the snow off her jacket and kick the slush off her boots.

"Lily, darling. I didn't think we'd see you today."

Lily smiled as a tall, willowy woman with ice-blond hair and huge black glasses approached. "Hi, Carole. I'm surprised I made it. The roads are horrible. But Frank told me he'd come up with an idea for hanging the nudes and I wanted to see what he had in mind."

Lily had never had a gallery show of her own art. In truth, the prospect of having people starting at her paintings, discussing them and even buying them made her tremble with fear.

"I am glad you stopped. You can help me label your invitations. And I wanted to double-check a few names you included on your guest list."

"Sure. I'm just going to take this painting back to Frank first. He was looking for something smaller and I thought this one might work."

Lily hurried through the warren of walls and display tables to the large workroom at the back of the store.

It was hard to believe that she was going to have her own show opening in just three weeks. She'd done her first painting just five months before, her creativity sparking to life during her affair with Tristan.

It had happened that way in the past, but she'd never been able to sustain the raw energy…until now. The day after he left camp, she'd picked up her brushes again and continued on with the nudes. She'd done a series of hands and after that, Daisy had posed for her, wrapped in brown craft paper.

"Frank?" she called.

A heavyset man appeared from behind a huge crate. "Hey, there, Lily. Didn't expect to see you today."

"I'm getting braver behind the wheel," she said. "I brought you the painting we discussed. If it's not right, let me know. I have a few others that I could finish."

Frank took the painting, deemed it acceptable, then gave Lily a rundown of how he wanted to show her exhibit. "The perfect thing to think about on a snowy night," she said.

As she turned to walk back to the front of the shop, Lily caught sight of a familiar canvas, propped against the opposite wall. She stared at it for a long moment, then crossed to remove it from the stack and set it in an empty spot where she might enjoy it.

It was the first nude she'd done of Tristan. It was still one of her favorite pieces and she hadn't quite resigned herself to selling it. But Carole had priced it higher than any of her other canvases.

Her mind spun back to the moment that she'd asked him to pose for her. Never had she expected it to return such an astounding reward. She felt like an artist now. Not to mention that he was a beautiful man with an incredible body. She seemed to think of him more and more often now that his paintings were about to go public.

"Carole, there is someone I'd like to add to the invitation list."

The other woman walked over to the desk and sat down, peering through her reading glasses at the screen. "All right. Name?"

"Tristan Quinn," she said.

"Oh, nice name," Carole cried. "Let me guess. Fashion model, sports star or pirate. I'll go with fashion model."

"No," Lily said. "He's a lawyer. He lives in one of those high-rise condos on the river."

"Don't worry, I'll track him down and make sure he gets an invitation. Anyone else?"

"You got the colony list, right?"

"I did. But you didn't include anyone from your family except your great-aunts."

"No, I won't be inviting anyone else. Just Violet, Daisy and Rose."

"Oh, I found something while I was searching through our photo archive for another project. Our gallery has been around since the early sixties." Carole pulled out a manila envelope and handed it to Lily.

Curious, Lily opened it and pulled out an 8 x 10 photo of the three Pigglestone sisters. They were standing together, each with a champagne flute in their hands.

"I would love to get another photo of them just like that one, posing with the champagne flutes," said Carole. "They'd be sure to print it in the Sunday arts section of the paper."

"I'm sure they'd enjoy that. This whole party is the highlight of their winter social season." Lily laughed. "It's the only thing that's on their social calendar, in fact."

"They must be so proud of you," Carole said.

"I'm kind of proud of myself," Lily said. She glanced down at the stack of invitations, then grabbed one. "I just had an idea. I want to deliver this personally."

"Darling, if you're going to deliver it today, you'd better go now or you'll get stuck in a snowdrift."

Lily hurried out of the gallery, pulling her scarf up around her face. The Mini was now completely covered with snow. Lily grabbed the brush from the front seat and cleared all the windows, then hopped in behind the wheel.

Though she had a GPS in the car, she remembered where she was going. She wound her way along the pier until she saw the building. Her heart stopped for a few seconds when she thought about what she was going to do. It didn't pay to think, Lily thought to herself. Besides, this was the perfect way to invite him. He couldn't refuse to come if he got a personal invitation.

She parked the car in the circular drive and hurried to the front door, skidding along the slippery sidewalk. When she opened the front door, the doorman stepped out from behind a desk.

"Hello," Lily said. "Can you tell me if Tristan Quinn is home? I have something I'd like to deliver to him."

"I can take it," the doorman said.

"I was hoping to deliver it personally," Lily said. "Could you call him and have him come down? If he's not home, I'll give it to you."

The doorman picked up the phone and punched in a few numbers. "Mr. Quinn, I have a delivery for you. The delivery person wants to give it to you personally." He paused. "A woman. Very pretty. Dark hair, kind of wavy. All right. Yes, sir."

The doorman set the phone down. "He says you can go on up. Number 1405. Fourteenth floor. Take a right off the elevator and go to the end of the hall."

"But I don't want to go up," she said. "I'd prefer it if he came down."

"It appears that he wants you to go up."

Lily thought about her options. Did she have the resolve to go upstairs? To stand in the hallway and explain her presence? To invite him to her party and then refuse the obligatory invitation inside? She wasn't so weak that she couldn't refuse. "Of course I could," she murmured. "I'll just hold it out and he'll have to—"

"Lily?"

She jumped at the sound of her name, then slowly

turned to face the elevator. Her breath seemed to catch in her throat and for a long moment, she couldn't draw another. Lily felt her face grow warm and flushed. Suddenly, the layers of clothes seemed to smother her.

"What are you doing here?"

Lily held out the envelope. "It's an invitation," she said. "To my gallery opening. I'm going to show the paintings that we did together and I thought you'd like to see them."

"What about your plans to go to Portugal?" he said.

"I decided not to go."

"How did you get here?"

"I drove," she said. "I'm legal now. I got my driver's license." Lily glanced outside. "I should really get going. The snow is getting worse." She held out the invitation again, praying he'd finally grab it. When he didn't, Lily handed it to the doorman. "I hope you'll come. It would be nice to have you there."

She hurried to the door, giving him a weak wave as she stepped out into the storm. Lily skidded back down the sidewalk to where the Mini was parked. When she heard him call her name again, she pretended she didn't hear. And when she pulled out onto the street, she nearly hit a parked car as the Mini swerved in the snow.

Her heart slammed in her chest and she felt giddy and light-headed. Lily pulled over to the curb and parked the car, waiting for her pulse to return to normal.

Groaning, she pitched forward, pressing her head against the steering wheel. For the past four months, she'd been imagining that exact moment when she saw Tristan again, when she'd have a chance to say something—anything—significant. But she'd never expected that she'd end up saying nothing.

"WHEN YOU CALLED and asked us to meet you at a bar on this side of town, I assumed it would be the kind of bar that we usually go to. What's with the artsy-fartsy place?" Jamie asked, peering at the customers that surrounded them. "All the people here look like they're on their way to the opera or some high-class art show."

Tristan followed his brother's gaze. It wasn't that bad, he thought to himself. And it was right across the street from the Welbrun Gallery. It was the perfect place to decide whether he was going to go to Lily's opening or not.

"I don't get a lot of time off," Thom said, "but I think we could have done better than this. They don't even have sports on television."

Thom, a hockey player, was off for the weekend due to the All-Star break, and Jamie was always happy to hang out with his two older brothers, but they usually found a place that served great craft beers, killer burgers and a wide selection of single women.

"I invited you here because it's closer to the gallery opening that we're going to later."

Thom frowned as he broke away from his study of the beer menu. "We're going to a gallery opening?" he asked. "Since when do we go to gallery openings? Malin doesn't even make me do that."

Thom and Malin had been together for nearly six

months and it was still a bit strange to hear him talk about her. The Quinn brothers had usually avoided long-term relationships. But this woman had captured his brother's heart and there was no indication that she was going to let him go. Thom freely admitted that he loved her and for the first time, Tristan understood exactly how he felt.

"Who is the artist?" Jamie asked.

"She's a client," Tristan replied.

"She's a *she*," Thom said, giving Jamie a knowing look. "This should be interesting."

"I'm not sure I want to go yet." Tristan asked. "This woman. It's…complicated."

"Is it ever not complicated with women?" Jamie asked. "That kind of goes with the whole dating thing."

"We're not dating. We haven't really seen each other since September. Except for a few days ago when she delivered the invitation."

"She personally delivers an invite and you're considering skipping the party?" Thom shook his head. "That's not cool."

"What kind of art is this?" Jamie asked. "Am I going to understand it, or am I just going to stand there and pretend that I understand it?"

"You'll understand some of it, I think," Tristan said. He reached out and grabbed his glass of bourbon, then took a sip. "She's kind of an amazing woman. I've never known anyone like her."

"That's what Thom says about Malin," Jamie said.

"It's true," Thom said.

Jamie chuckled. "Who would have thought a Quinn

brother would have turned out to be some fairy-tale prince? Or is it a white knight?"

"It's not that way," Thom said. "The prince is the one who saves the princess. Malin saved me, I didn't save her. I was the beast, she was the beauty." He glanced over at Tristan. "What about you?"

"I still haven't figured it all out yet. I'll let you know when I can apply a metaphor. I can't very well be the prince, though. More like the pauper. She's got all the money."

"How much?" Jamie asked.

Tristan shrugged. "I'm not sure. I think maybe millions?"

His brothers both gasped. "That could be a problem."

"I used to believe so. But the real issue was that I wasn't sure whether she really wanted me. Whether she believed we could have a life together. But maybe now she's ready to take that leap."

"Is there going to be food at this party?" Thom asked. "Because if there is, I say we go over there right now and hit it hard."

Tristan drew a deep breath and nodded. "You're here for support, all right? Not to screw around, not to inhale the buffet or insult the guests."

"You're the pauper. You need the free food," Thom chided.

"This is important to Lily and if you mess up, I'm going beat the crap out of you."

"He hasn't beat us up in years," Thom said. "I think he overestimates his skills as a fighter."

They finished their drinks, paid the bartender, then strolled across the street to the gallery, hurrying against the sub-zero cold. As they walked through the tall plate glass doors, an attendant took their coats and handed them each a ticket. Tristan observed the room as he straightened his tie, searching the crowd for Lily's slender body and beautiful face.

Compared to the people in the bar, the patrons in the gallery were subdued. A few people turned to look at them as they walked inside, including Lily. She spotted Tristan from across the room, their gazes meeting, then lingering for a long moment. He held his breath as she slowly crossed the room.

"Hi, Tristan," she murmured, giving him a quick kiss on the cheek.

"Hi, Lily. You look amazing."

"I'm wearing underwear!" she whispered.

"No, that's not it. I think it's the dress," he said. Tristan took her hand and twirled her around. Low-cut at the neck and high-cut along the leg, the dress was sewn with thousands of tiny crystals that glittered in the light. It was so close to the color of her skin that from a distance, she looked as though she were naked and dipped in sugar crystals. He fought the urge to drag her outside, find a quiet shadow and kiss her until she couldn't take any more. But it was cold and she had other guests to attend to. He was one of many guests that she had to please.

"I brought my brothers along," Tristan said. "This is Thom and Jamie."

Lily held out her hand. "It's a pleasure to meet you

both. Has Tristan told you about the nudes?" Lily looked over at him. "No?" She smiled. "I'd start there and work your way forward." She leaned close and gave Tristan another kiss on the cheek. "We'll talk later."

"So, there are nudes," Jamie murmured as they walked to the rear of the gallery. "This is already better than I thought it would be."

"It's about to get even better," Tristan warned him.

They stood in front of the largest canvas, almost seven feet tall. It was the one Lily had been working on when he'd left, a full frontal view. His face was hidden by the shadows and the painting had elements of the abstract, but Tristan still recognized his own body.

"Wow," Thom said. "Now there's a fella who's been blessed by the gods."

"If I had that underneath my boxers, I'd be walking around naked all the time," Jamie added.

"Shut up," Tristan said. "This isn't porn, it's art."

"What are you getting all bent about?" Jamie asked. "Is it 'cause your girl spent time with Mr. Studly there when she should have been spending time with you?"

Thom cleared his throat. "Jamie? I don't think that's it."

"What isn't it?"

"That picture there? I believe that's a picture of our very own brother, Tristan Quinn. Am I right?"

Tristan nodded. "Yeah, that's me. And so are all the others. Except the women."

"Jesus," Jamie gasped. "You're a brave one to let all your bits and pieces out for the world to see."

"No one knows it's me," he said. "And I'm not ashamed. The paintings are really good."

"They are," Thom said. "You should be proud. Of her, not you. Not too many people can do something like this."

"Tristan? Is that you?"

The Pigglestone sisters appeared from behind a gallery panel. The moment they saw him, they rushed up with hugs and kisses. "Ladies, I'd like you to meet my brothers, Thom and Jamie. Boys, this is Violet, Daisy and Rose Pigglestone. They're Lily's great-aunts. They own the artists' colony where I met Lily."

"We didn't expect to see you this weekend."

"Lily hand-delivered an invitation. I couldn't refuse."

"And now that you've seen her again, how do you feel?" Violet asked. "Have you missed her? I know she's missed you."

"Vi, you shouldn't speak for Lily. You can't be sure that's true. You only wish it was." Rose took his hand. "We've definitely missed you, though."

"I've missed you, too," he said. "I miss the warm weather and the sound of the water lapping at the shore of the lake and the smell of barbecue on the breeze."

"You must come back next summer," Rose said.

"Maybe I will," Tristan said.

The ladies wandered off and Tristan's brothers followed, heading for the buffet table. He moved along the rear wall, observing each painting, taking in the beautiful colors and details that Lily had put on the canvas.

"I wish we had time to talk." Lily slipped her arm through his and Tristan smiled.

"I think your paintings speak for themselves."

"You like them?"

"I do. I'm not sure I understand everything I should about them, but I they're wonderful. You're a great artist."

"What did your brothers say?" Lily asked.

"They were pretty impressed," Tristan replied.

"With the paintings? Or the subject?"

He chuckled. "It's hard to say." Though they were chatting about the show, Tristan couldn't keep his thoughts off the sweet scent of her perfume and the way her hair fell across her face. He wanted to pull her into his arms and kiss her.

"The reviews have been good," she said. "And sales have been positive. I never thought this would be possible. It's because of you that it happened. You gave me the courage and the confidence."

"I took my clothes off and let you sketch me," he said, "and that's about all I did."

Lily shook her head. "When I was little, I used to think if I could find a four-leaf clover that I would make a beautiful drawing that day. And then I got it in my head that blueberries made me more talented. After that, it was sable brushes. I had to buy the most expensive brushes. And then I was convinced that I couldn't paint until I was involved in a passionate affair. So I met you and I started painting. But then you left and I continued to paint and paint and I couldn't stop. Even without you."

"That's great to hear," Tristan said.

They stood in silence for a long moment staring at each other, their eyes locked. Tristan reached out and brushed his fingertips along her cheek and Lily closed her eyes. "You should probably go," Lily murmured. "I find myself wanting to spend the rest of the evening all alone with you."

"When this is finished and you've sold all your paintings," Tristan asked, "maybe we can go out and get something to eat?"

"Like a date?" Lily asked.

"Yeah, like a date. Would there be anything wrong with that?"

"That's the kind of thing two normal adults do, isn't it? We've never really followed that rule book, but I suppose we could always give it a try." She paused. "Do you love me, Tristan Quinn?"

"I do," he said.

"And how do you know?"

"Because it doesn't matter how much time we spend apart. When I'm with you, I feel like I'm home. And I've never really had a place like that until now."

"I feel exactly the same. I love you, too, Tristan. And now I belive that I always will. I have to get back to my guests," she said. "But if you hang around, I'll find you a little later."

"I was thinking I could go home and you could find me there?"

"Would you make me a nice, hot bath?"

"I will."

"And will you rub my feet?"

"I will."

"Then I'll be there."

Tristan took her face between his hands and he gave her a gentle kiss. "I'll see you, later, Lily."

She began to walk away, then turned to face him. "I think we have this relationship thing down," she said.

"We just might," Tristan replied.

She threw him a kiss and then disappeared into the crowd. A few seconds later, his brothers rejoined him. Thom threw his arm over Tristan's shoulder. "I can see where this is going," he muttered.

"Me, too," Tristan said. "For the rest of my life."

Epilogue

THE WEATHER STATION called it the biggest blizzard of
the season. The snow had started falling that morning
and by the time the sun went down, the trees around
Fence Lake were bent under the weight of the snow.

Lily stood next to the doors leading out to the lake.
She'd winterized the stone cottage earlier that fall and
even the most stubborn drafts were dissolved by a cozy,
warm heat.

She heard footsteps on the front porch and hurried
over to open the door. Tristan, dressed in a hooded
parka and boots, stood at the door, his arms piled high
with firewood.

"Is this enough?"

"Come in," she said, tugging on his sleeve as snow
swirled around her feet.

He did as he was told and she slammed the door behind him. "How deep is it?"

"Two feet. Some of the drifts are up to my waist.
It's going to get worse. The Mini might be buried until
spring. You should never have bought such a short car."

Lily helped Tristan out of his coat, brushing off the snow before hanging the jacket on a peg beside the door. Then he sat down on a bench and kicked off his boots. "It's hard to believe we were running around naked just six months ago."

"We can still run around naked," Lily said.

He growled softly and slipped his hands around her waist. Lily snuggled up against him, the warmth of him seeping through his fleece shirt. "So naked first, lunch second?"

"We'll need our energy to stay warm," Lily said. "We should have lunch first."

She took his hand and pulled him along to the kitchen. She'd made a huge pot of soup that morning and purchased a pair of baguettes from a French bakery near Tristan's condo in St. Paul.

Lily turned the stove on to heat the soup. Then she flipped on the oven to warm the bread. "Should I open a bottle of wine?"

"Something wicked?"

"Absolutely. Maybe we'll try someplace new, like the desk."

"Don't you think it's a little strange that we're christening every spot in this cottage?"

"No," Tristan said. "It's winter in Minnesota. We can go ice fishing, we can play cards or we can have sex."

Lily leaned back against the edge of the counter. "I've never been ice fishing," she said, a teasing smile on her face.

"I'll clear the desk."

"There's so many papers stacked there. Just—"

Before she could plead with him to be neat, Tristan swept his arm across the scarred oak surface. Papers few into the air and scattered on the floor.

"No!" Lily screamed.

He reached for the battered blotter and tossed it up in the air. But his disposal of the last item on the desk was enough to cause the both of them to freeze. A small pile of papers sat on the center of the desk, previously hidden by the blotter. Lily slowly approached from the kitchen. From Lily's viewpoint the sheaf of documents looked like something very legal. Tristan stood back from the table, his arms crossed over his chest. "It's a deed," he said.

"No," Lily said.

"I've seen them before. It's a deed."

Lily snatched the papers up holding her breath. "It does say deed. But who is it deeded to?"

He took the papers from her fingers and crossed to the sofa, sitting down across from the fire. Lily watched his face, looking for the slightest clue to his reaction. She sat down beside him and held tight to his arm.

"This is it," Tristan finally said. "This is a transfer of deed from your great-grandfather Edward Pigglestone, to his three daughters—Violet, Daisy and Rose. Here's the description of the property. Seven-hundred seventy acres including the five-hundred-thirty-nine acre Fence Lake. Look at the date he signed it."

"Two days before he died. He was going to file it and then he must have—" She drew a ragged breath.

"Is this what we need to win the case for good?" Lily asked.

Tristan smiled. "I think it is. This should prove Edward's intention to leave the property to the sisters."

Lily felt tears flooding her eyes, but they were accompanied by uncontrollable laughter. She threw her arms around Tristan's neck. He picked her up and spun her around. Then he carried her over to the desk and set her down.

"I think this is our happy ending," he said.

"And they lived happily ever after," Lily said. "In a tiny stone cottage by a pretty blue lake."

There would be time later to tell the sisters and to contact all their friends. But for now Lily wanted to stay safe inside the cottage, away from the wind and the snow, and imagine the long life that awaited her with Tristan at her side.

* * * * *

COMING NEXT MONTH FROM

Available October 18, 2016

#915 CHRISTMAS WITH THE MARINE
Uniformly Hot! • by Candace Havens

Ben Hawthorne is a Marine on a mission when he runs into Ainsley Garrett, his very own Christmas miracle. Focused on their careers, neither wants a relationship. Even if the chemistry between them would make Santa blush!

#916 HER NAUGHTY HOLIDAY
Men at Work • by Tiffany Reisz

Erick Fields is shocked when prim and proper Clover Greene agrees that sex should be part of their "fake boyfriend" deal. She needed a buffer against her judgmental family, but this Thanksgiving she's getting a whole lot more!

#917 HOT WINTER NIGHTS
Made in Montana • by Debbi Rawlins

For the first time in his life, sexy rancher Clint Landers is on the naughty list... But if it's up to Lila Loveridge, he'll get everything he wished for this Christmas.

#918 CHRISTMAS IN HIS BED
by Sasha Summers

When Tatum Buchanan suggests to Spencer Ryan that they spend the twelve nights before Christmas in bed, no strings attached, he agrees. But can he let her go on December 25?

REQUEST YOUR FREE BOOKS!
2 FREE NOVELS PLUS 2 FREE GIFTS!

ℍ HARLEQUIN®

Blaze®

r e d - h o t   r e a d s !

YES! Please send me 2 FREE Harlequin® Blaze® novels and my 2 FREE gifts (gifts are worth about $10). After receiving them, if I don't wish to receive any more books, I can return the shipping statement marked "cancel." If I don't cancel, I will receive 4 brand-new novels every month and be billed just $4.74 per book in the U.S. or $5.21 per book in Canada. That's a savings of at least 14% off the cover price. It's quite a bargain. Shipping and handling is just 50¢ per book in the U.S. and 75¢ per book in Canada.* I understand that accepting the 2 free books and gifts places me under no obligation to buy anything. I can always return a shipment and cancel at any time. Even if I never buy another book, the two free books and gifts are mine to keep forever.

150/350 HDN GH2D

Name _____ (PLEASE PRINT) _____

Address _____ Apt. # _____

City _____ State/Prov. _____ Zip/Postal Code _____

Signature (if under 18, a parent or guardian must sign) _____

Mail to the **Reader Service:**
IN U.S.A.: P.O. Box 1867, Buffalo, NY 14240-1867
IN CANADA: P.O. Box 609, Fort Erie, Ontario L2A 5X3

Want to try two free books from another line?
Call 1-800-873-8635 or visit www.ReaderService.com.

* Terms and prices subject to change without notice. Prices do not include applicable taxes. Sales tax applicable in N.Y. Canadian residents will be charged applicable taxes. Offer not valid in Quebec. This offer is limited to one order per household. Not valid for current subscribers to Harlequin Blaze books. All orders subject to credit approval. Credit or debit balances in a customer's account(s) may be offset by any other outstanding balance owed by or to the customer. Please allow 4 to 6 weeks for delivery. Offer available while quantities last.

Your Privacy—The Reader Service is committed to protecting your privacy. Our Privacy Policy is available online at www.ReaderService.com or upon request from the Reader Service.

We make a portion of our mailing list available to reputable third parties that offer products we believe may interest you. If you prefer that we not exchange your name with third parties, or if you wish to clarify or modify your communication preferences, please visit us at www.ReaderService.com/consumerschoice or write to us at Reader Service Preference Service, P.O. Box 9062, Buffalo, NY 14240-9062. Include your complete name and address.

HB15

SPECIAL EXCERPT FROM

◆HARLEQUIN

Blaze

Erick Fields is shocked when prim and proper Clover Greene agrees that sex should be part of their "fake boyfriend" deal. She needed a buffer against her judgmental family, but this Thanksgiving she's getting a whole lot more!

Read on for a sneak preview of
HER NAUGHTY HOLIDAY,
book three of Tiffany Reisz's sexy holiday trilogy
MEN AT WORK.

"I'm not going to try to convince you to do something you don't want to do," Clover said.

"Why not?"

"Because no means no."

"I didn't say no. Come on. I'm a businessman. Let's haggle."

Clover laughed a nervous laugh, almost a giggle. She sat behind her desk and Erick sat on the desk next to her.

"You're pretty when you laugh," he said. "But you're also pretty when you don't laugh."

"You're sweet," she said. "I feel like I shouldn't have brought this up."

"So do you really need someone to play boyfriend for the week? It's that bad with your family?"

She sighed heavily and sat back.

"It's hard," she said. "They love me but that doesn't make the stuff they say easier to hear. They think they'r saying 'We love you and we want you to be happy,' but what I hear is 'You're inadequate, you're a disappointment and you haven't done what you're supposed to do to make *us* happy.'"

He grinned at her and shrugged. "You think I'm cute?" he asked.

"You're hot," she said. "Like UPS-driver hot."

"That's hot."

"Smoking."

"This is fun," he said. "Why haven't we ever flirted with each other before?"

"You know, my parents would probably be very impressed if they thought I were dating a single father. They'd think that was a ready-made family."

"You really want me to be your boyfriend?" Erick asked. He already planned on doing it. He'd do anything for this woman, including but not limited to pretending to be her boyfriend for a couple days.

"I would appreciate it," she said.

"We can have sex all week, too, right?"

"Okay."

"What?" Erick burst into laughter.

"What?" she repeated. "Why are you laughing?"

"I didn't think you'd say yes. I was joking."

"You were?" Her blue eyes went wide.

"Well…yeah. I mean, not that I don't want to. I do want to. I swear to God, I thought you'd say no. I never guessed you'd say yes, not in a million years."

"And why not?"

Don't miss HER NAUGHTY HOLIDAY
by Tiffany Reisz, available November 2016 wherever
Harlequin® Blaze® books and ebooks are sold.

Reading Has Its Rewards

Earn **FREE BOOKS!**

Register at **Harlequin My Rewards** and submit your Harlequin purchases from wherever you shop to earn points for free books and other exclusive rewards.

Plus submit your purchases from now till May 30th for a chance to win a $500 Visa Card*.

Visit **HarlequinMyRewards.com** today

MYR16

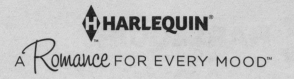

JUST CAN'T GET ENOUGH?

Join our social communities
and talk to us online.

You will have access to the latest
news on upcoming titles and special
promotions, but most importantly,
you can talk to other fans about your
favorite Harlequin reads.

Harlequin.com/Community